The Priest's Boy

The Priest's Boy

By Clive Doucet

Black Moss Press

Published by Black Moss Press
2450 Byng Rd., Windsor, Ontario
N8W 3E8.

Black Moss Books are distributed in Canada
and the United States by Firefly Books, Ltd., 250 Sparks Avenue,
Willowdale, Ontario, M2H 2S4.

Financial assistance toward publication of this book was gratefully
received from the Canada Council and the
Ontario Arts Council.

Cover art by Tim Dixon

Typesetting and page design by Kristina Russelo

Printed and bound in Canada by Hignell Printing Ltd.,
Winnipeg, Manitoba.

Canadian Cataloguing in Publication Data
Doucet, Clive, 1946-
The priest's boy

ISBN 0-88753-236-5

I. Title

PS8557.0787P74 1992   C813'.54   C92-090000-3
PR919.3.D69P74 1992

Contents

To some of my favourite seal hunters

Michael Geiger, Karine Rogers, Sean Connors,
Emma and Julian Doucet

Preface

Imagine a narrow, gravel road that sweeps along the seacoast. The road is balanced on the edge of cliffs between green fields and the ocean curving out to the horizon. The fields are narrow, hillside holdings and give way to green mountains that defy sea and sky. It is a powerful landscape that permits human habitation but does not welcome it.

The road takes you across a narrow bridge and then ever further into the mountains. You pass an inlet of the sea, no more than a cove. Scattered around the edges of this little harbour are fishermen's cabins. Nets are splayed out, drying in the sun. The smell of salt and fish impregnates the air of the little harbour. There is a wharf along one shore which opens onto a large, nondescript shed that serves as a fish plant and lobster cannery. On the wharf, there are men splitting cod. A cloud of white and grey seagulls gathers about their heads waiting for the offal.

In the evening, there are so many boats in the cove that you can walk from one shore to the other without getting your feet wet. The boats are small, wooden dories for one or two fishermen. This is the harbour of St. Joseph de la Mer. It is the last village but one, before the road strikes the highlands and the mountains begin in earnest.

It is 1937 during the time of the Great Depression. There is no money in the village and there has been none for what seems like forever. The people of St. Joseph de la Mer have been thrown entirely on themselves. Every inch of land that can be ploughed has been seeded for potatoes and turnips and grain. Every mountain meadow that can support a cow or a sheep is grazed. Every boat that can be used for fishing is caulked and put upon the sea. Nothing is wasted.

Up from the harbour, between the sea and the mountains, the village itself spreads out along the coast in a long line of small farms. The distance from one end of the village to the other is not much more than two miles, two miles, fifty-two houses, two one-room schools, one store, one blacksmith, one post-office, one church, and six hundred souls.

It is a world where there is no indoor plumbing, few radios, fewer cars and little travel. Television does not exist. You can walk into anyone's home without fear of interrupting a television program. Talk is the spice of life. It is as if the village is one enormous conversation and each house is just another part of the same conversation. Folk tales hadn't become folk tales yet. They were just homemade stories people told to amuse themselves. Now, they are called folk tales because no one can quite remember who first told the story or why. They are thought of as quaint, as if in the days before television people were a little simple.

The church is a white, clapboard building, with its back towards the sea and the steeple facing the mountains. The church is apart from the village on a raise of land that leaves it visible from everywhere but the harbour, as if the business of gutting fish and praying were not compatible. Father Simon Aucoin stands at the door of his little church. His white vestments snapping about him in the wind so that he fills the entire doorway. It is April and the smell of the land reviving from the long winter freeze is everywhere.

The priest turns and enters his church leaving nothing but a dark, colourless, vacuum at the door, pulling people to follow him. The altar boy rings the steeple bell for the last time. Without the repetition, the sound of the bell diminishes into the ocean air as if it has been evaporated, to be replaced by nothing but the quiet shuffle of people taking their seats.

Spring is a difficult time in Cape Breton and April is the worst month of all. The whole world has begun to get cabin fever. The women are fed up with the men. The men are fed up with the women. Everyone wants to be gone. The farmers to get out on the land. The fishermen to get out on the sea. The women to get out of the kitchen. But no one can move. The land is too wet to work. The ice still groans on the sea in soft pulpy, pack ice over the fishing grounds. Everyone must wait. Wait for the roads to dry. Wait for the ewes to lamb, the cows to calf. It is a cranky, dangerous time. The young priest can feel it as he prepares himself for Mass. He opens his hands slowly, trying to gather some energy to counter the angry force which comes against him.

"In nomine Patris, et Filii, et Spiritus Sanctus Sancti. Amen."

He waits listening to his voice. It doesn't fill the church with the satisfying sounds of a good bass profundo. The priest has nothing more than a light tenor which he has to husband carefully. He waits. This hesitancy annoys the congregation. They want him to sing through the Mass quickly today. To make them forget that it is April and not cold enough to be winter and yet not warm enough to be spring.

The young priest bites at his lower lip and it comes to him that he can do nothing; nothing except to say the Mass.

"I will go unto the Altar of God. To God the joy of my youth."

This time his voice is reasonable. It is light but carries clearly towards the balcony. The Ordinary of the Mass has begun.

Philibert Guarantees

"Chacun à son métier et les vaches seront bien gardées."

Marriage is a fool's game, that is the long and short of it. It makes people laugh when I tell them that, and the more vehement I become, the more examples of disaster that I give, the more interested they become. *"Philibert, tu as plus d'oeufs dans ton panier que ça,"* they say.

Yes, I've got more eggs in the basket, but not the ones they think. I've got a young man who was widowed last fall with four young children, all younger than yours. He is poor, poor, poor. He lost his boat in a storm. There is not a penny in that poor man's house. He is a man born to woe and I'll tell you something, he's going to marry the school mistress who has fallen in love with him. She has been watching the way he struggles into Mass each Sunday. The children are always decked out in their one and only best attire. His black hair is slicked down and she thinks to herself that he needs her; that he has potential to be something more than a fisherman's helper.

Nonsense, I know the man, he is one of those obliging souls who must always appear that he is on the right side of God's ledger. The kind that turns poverty into a virtue and ineptitude into grace. I think that his first wife became so tired of his cloying saintliness, she preferred a quick death to a long purgatory. Of course, I've warned the teacher, but what good does it do? He smiles, and she crumbles.

Mark my words, the school teacher will marry him in March as sure as I'm sitting here. No doubt, she will soon after be pregnant, lose her job and then she will join him on poverty row. For this trouble, I will get a fat fee.

Myself, I prefer to read the newspaper and drink good strong tea. Newspapers don't talk back to you. They don't ask why the living room isn't wallpapered or when was the last time you changed your socks. My own wife, God bless her, used to screech every time that I picked up the newspaper. It got so I could not sit down without her howling 'Philibert! Philibert! Where are you?' as if she could not see where I was.

One day in a fit of desperation, I went next door to my neighbours where they would let me read in peace. It turned out old Monsieur Leblanc could not read a word, so I read to him. As soon as I had done this little thing, the Leblancs who as everyone knows are the salt of the earth, gave me a loaf of bread as payment. This pleased my wife who hates baking and so I managed to kill two birds with one stone. I read the paper in peace and I pleased my wife.

It got to be known that I would read the newspaper to those who could not read and soon I began to have a regular, little reading circuit. In this way I earned a little money. At the same time, I began to carry messages about, Arthur à William would like to meet Sophie à John after church and the like. It was not something I asked to do, I did not choose to be a matchmaker, people chose me and soon I was stuck with it. People expected me to suggest a companion for a grieving widow or a nice, young man for their shy daughter. To be perfectly honest, there are easier ways to make a living, like sticking your head in the jaws of a crocodile.

But, it's not all bad, there are some good things to my *métier*. Ever since I began travelling, my wife has been quite content. She says the house is quite pleasant now. She's rarely cranky. This is the best sort of marriage. You see your wife only occasionally and when you do, you remember to praise her lavishly. Praise, praise, praise, that is the only thing a wife will bear. Yes, I always counsel youngsters that if they are considering marriage, the best approach is not to.

See, what did I tell you. Here's an article in the newspaper that says exactly that. I must read it to you. It's about an Englishman in Sydney. You know the rich kind that have a dog and go for walks on Sunday because they've done nothing all week. It says here this Englishman's son fell in love with an Indian girl from Whycocomaugh. The father was enraged with the boy and the son ran away to be with the girl who from all accounts is very beautiful. There is a picture of her here. Yes, I would say that she is beautiful, wouldn't you? Look at the way her hair falls in waves and the soft look to her eyes. No, I wouldn't kick her out of bed.

The son must have thought so also because he rushed off to Whycocomaugh to marry the Indian girl, but the father found out, and he chased after the lad with his chauffeur. They found him on the road to Whycocomaugh and the two of them pounced on the boy, tied him up hand and foot and drove him back to Sydney. He was delivered right on to one of the steel boats and shipped out to Britain like so much rough baggage.

Is that the end of the story? Who knows? What will the Indian girl do? What will the English boy do? I don't know. I guess we'll just have to watch the paper. But no doubt the father did the right thing. Love is a terrible reason to get married.

If it is not love then what is it?

Ahh, that is the thing, I don't know. I've seen educated women marry illiterate farmers and the marriage be as happy as daisies on a spring day. I've seen the same thing turn into disaster where the one is always cranking at the stupidity of the other. I've seen parents take against the marriage of children like this walking stick Englishman and be wrong, wrong, wrong and I've seen them predict disaster perfectly. Who knows where marriages are made? Certainly not me, I'm just a fool who goes around reading the newspaper. I would not put the slightest trust in anything I say.

"Philibert, I never said I wanted to meet Isabet à Marcellin."

"Good, because Isabet à Marcellin is a menace. She drove her first husband to an early grave. Nothing that he ever did was good enough for her. She is in my humble view the worst kind of woman, ambitious for herself but unwilling to do much about it, and so she looks at the world 'à travers.' Like her first husband, the world is never quite good enough for her.

"No, you are quite right not to be interested. I would not marry the widow from Plateau either, not if you gave me all the tea in China. Not that she would marry me. I'm sure that she wouldn't. A poor Matchmaker would not be good enough for Isabet à Marcellin and nor, fortunately, are you. You have too many children and your health is not good enough, that is the long and short of it. You're wise to look elsewhere."

"But I don't wish to look anywhere. Six sons and one wife are enough for any man."

"In case you hadn't noticed, cher ami, Marie has passed away and your boys need a woman around the house. It's not natural to be alone with a houseful of children. Even the priest has a housekeeper. No, it's not natural. When you get right down to it, even Isabet à Marcellin is better than being alone. Maybe she's good in bed. There must be a good side to her, somewhere. If you want my advice, Marcel."

"Which you'll give me whether I want it or not."

"Ahh, you know me too well. It's not complicated. My advice is simple. Find someone who does not expect you to be more than you are. An old school chum, someone who can curl up in your arms and laugh. Someone who is a little chubby. Chubby women are usually, although not always, more agreeable than thin ones, someone with a little property, someone with a sense of humour. Not that I guarantee anything, Philibert guarantees nothing but *emmerdement*. It's just the depth that I'm contesting.

"See! See! I made you smile. It's not a rumour, Marcel Boudreau can smile! Smile more and I guarantee women will be beating a path to your front door, but first you must get well. You must get rid of that cough. It sounds consumptive. You must keep the house warmer. It's freezing in here. And get yourself spruced up. It's no good coming to Mass as if you've been in bed sick all week. You need colour in your cheeks and a glint in your eye. You can't mourn forever. Your boys need a mother and you need a wife."

"They have a place."

"Then why did you send me to see Father Aucoin about Daniel?"

"Why shouldn't I? He's musical. Father Aucoin is musical. I have nothing here. A wife will not give me a piano. The priest can teach Daniel, just like he did for Robert."

"I put the question to him, delicately."

"Well?"

"He said yes. I checked with my sainted cousin and he said it would be fine. Guaranteed. If you want, we can bring him to the Presbytery tomorrow. No doubt, Daniel will be a great success there. And no doubt, Marie Laure will be madder than a hatter when she discovers it's another Boudreau boy and not one of her large sons who's staying at the Presbytery, but that's life. God love us look at the time! Goodbye old friend, if you like, I'll leave the paper."

.

The Windows

The Postmistress of St. Joseph de la Mer could see the windows from the door of the Post Office. In the evening, the warm yellow panes glowed from the top of harbour hill for all to see. It gave one the shivers that anyone could be so brazen. The Postmistress began to complain. First, she complained to her husband, who nodded politely and went out to the barn to milk. Then she went next door to complain to Genevieve. Genevieve talked it over with her daughter Sylvie and Sylvie talked it over with her best friend Marie-Laure. Marie-Laure told Sylvie, she had seen little boys lined up at Marguerite Poirier's window peering in to see what they could see.

On Sunday, at the church door, the Postmistress, Marie-Laure, Sylvie, and Genevieve clustered about Father Aucoin like a delegation of chunky angels. Their bosoms heaved. Their eyes sparked indignation and their stomachs flattened. Something had to be done. Father Aucoin listened, inclined his head slightly, tightened his lips and a small, deep line began to crease the bridge of his nose.

It was understood that a few days later a hand-written note went from the Presbytery down the road to the harbour and up the hill to Marguerite Poirier. The note politely requested Marguerite Poirier to hang blinds on her windows and to attend Mass on Sunday. It was signed Simon Aucoin, R.P.

The Postmistress, Marie-Laure, Sylvie and Genevieve waited for the blinds to cover the patches of butter yellow and the little house on the hill to disappear into the penumbra of a Cape Breton winter night. But, January days drifted into February and blinds were not hung to hide the windows. They continued to shine luminously over the harbour. Nor did Marguerite Poirier come to mass and certain men continued to visit Marguerite Poirier and certain little boys continued to creep up the hill to peer in and see what they could see.

Now all this was puzzling to the parishioners of St. Joseph de la Mer because their priest was not a man who believed heaven was a place for the self-indulgent. The celestial ladder could only be climbed through stern and unrelenting vigilance, and he was quick to draw the laggards up whether they wanted to go or not. In short, Father Aucoin did not trust the mortal coil. With the exception of weddings, he frowned on dancing for it offered the occasion for sin. Nor did he care for the excessive walking among the younger folk. He encouraged them to be modest, work hard at their studies, sing in the church choir and concentrate on the care of their eternal soul. In this way, they might avoid the occasion for sin and attain the grace of eternal life.

Marguerite Poirier was clearly not trying to avoid the occasion for sin and the Postmistress waited confidently for the wrath of Father Aucoin to fall about her head.

Nothing happened. Father Aucoin did not preach from the pulpit against Marguerite Poirier. He did not speak about 'purging out the leaven of malice with the unleavened bread of sincerity and truth.' He did not visit Marguerite Poirier's. He did not speak quietly to certain persons. He did nothing and the news began to run like a small, malignant ripple from the Post Office of St. Joseph de la Mer.

Father Aucoin seemed unaware of the unrest in his Parish. He continued on his daily round. He began the day with the seven o'clock Mass, taught Cathecism and Latin between 9 and 11, said the Angelus at noon, heard confessions in the afternoon. And confessions with Father Aucoin remained a hard-felt thing. Tough, old lumberjacks swore off liquor for a few months. Miscreant boys promised to clean up their vocabulary. Father Côté from Margaree Forks and Father Rory from Inverness came once a month to visit their confessions on Father Aucoin which was a source of pride to the parishioners of St. Joseph de la Mer.

Like a schoolboy himself, Father Aucoin said his own prayers each night before he went to bed. And just in case he should be caught idle, he read from his breviary as he walked from presbytery to church. An endless river of prayers flowed out of the windows of the little church in St. Joseph de la Mer towards heaven beseeching God for this and forgiveness for that. But all the priest's prayers did not hang curtains on Marguerite Poirier's windows. Each evening, they glowed in the winter night from the top of harbour hill. And when the confessions had worn off, miscreant boys sneaked up the hill to peer in the windows to see what they could see.

One evening when Father Aucoin was sitting down to supper, a fisherman's wife arrived at the door of the Presbytery. She had been crying and her tears had frozen against her cheeks. She was wearing a thin, cloth coat against the winter wind and she shivered like a child, but she would not come inside the Presbytery, instead she stood crying and stamping her feet at the door. The new tears melting the old.

Now, this woman did not consider it her business to know about the sins of others. She came to Mass each Sunday. Her children sat beside her scrubbed and shorn. Her husband, who had a beautiful voice, sang in the church choir. In short, her family was a pillar of the community. Father Aucoin inclined his head and tightened his lips, a small line appeared at the bridge of his nose and as she talked, he nodded sympathetically. But still the woman would not come out of the cold winter wind. When she could talk no more, she dried her eyes and left feeling a little better.

Father Aucoin did not go to the church to pray. He did not finish his supper. He changed his old soutane for an equally decrepit one, pulled on his good wool coat, the one his brother had sent him from Boston, and then left the Presbytery on foot. He did not take his breviary. He leaned into the wind and walked as fast as he could along the sea cliffs towards the harbour of St. Joseph de la Mer. The wind clawed at his good coat spiking shafts of chill air against his chest and drawing tears from his eyes. Beneath the cliffs the winter ice creaked and groaned against the shore in slow, perpetual motion.

Marguerite Poirier lived in a small house on top of the hill which overlooked the harbour. It was not much more than a wood shed with a stove and bed. In a larger community than St. Joseph de la Mer, Marguerite might have been called a whore. But in St. Joseph de la Mer, she was not quite that. She was a widow who had remarried in a sentimental fit to a poor man, but after the fit had passed, had decided that she did not much care for him. Since that time, it was widely known that if you were a man troubled with a certain disposition, Marguerite Poirier might help you. And so when her second husband left, there would always be a visitor at Marguerite Poirier's. They gathered like Tom cats at her door.

All this was known in the Presbytery as well as on the dock of St. Joseph de la Mer. Father Aucoin received daily reports from a number of busy-bodies who made it their business to tell the priest everything that happened in the parish. He knew who had burnt their thumb while cooking; who had sold ten barrels of herring to Robin-Jones, but had delivered only nine; which women were expecting; whose cows had been put down with T.B.; who had had a prosperous fishing season and who had not. There was, in short, very little that happened in St. Joseph de la Mer which Father Aucoin did not know and what he did not know, he organised. But he did not know Marguerite Poirier. He could not recognise Marguerite by her stride or the lilt of her voice.

She was a stranger to him and he walked up to her little house with a feeling of unease. As the little, yellow window panes grew larger, his own uncertainty grew. He knocked at her kitchen door, but no one responded. He found himself shivering. He knocked again until his knuckles hurt, but still there was no response and not knowing what else to do, he peered nervously like a small boy through the window beside the door.

Inside, he saw a wood stove, just as it had been described to him. A wood box was on the other side of the stove. In front of the stove was a rocking chair and a bright kerosene lamp hung over the table, but he saw no one. The house appeared to be empty.

"What do you want?" The question came at Father Aucoin in a strong, fierce voice from directly behind him. Surprised, he swung around in a guilty, jerking motion to face Marguerite Poirier. She was carrying a large armload of wood and this blocked almost the entire view of her.

"I would like to speak to you," said Father Aucoin.

"Then open the door and go in."

Father Aucoin did as he was told.

Marguerite Poirier followed him into her kitchen and deposited her armload of wood with a crash into the wood box. She turned to face him brushing chips of wood from the front of her dress. She was a small woman with a strong, female figure, thick, dark hair, a straight Norman nose, a firm chin and a pale, chiselled face which was all planes. In a different situation, she would have been considered beautiful. As it was, she was simply Marguerite Poirier.

Curiously, both the woman and the priest were dressed much the same way, the priest in his worn, black soutane and Marguerite in an equally worn, black dress that buttoned high on the throat and fell to the ankles. Except for the white dog collar around the priest's neck, there was not a spot of colour in either of their attire. Marguerite folded her arms just under her breasts and waited for the priest to speak. She did not ask him to sit down. She waited.

Father Aucoin's hand went to his forehead in a nervous reflex which he always followed when he wasn't sure what to do. Marguerite did not move. Her breath came and went in calm, relaxed motions causing her breasts to rise and fall slightly under her tight dress.

"I came to see about putting curtains on your windows," said Father Aucoin finally getting the thought out into words.

"Why should I get curtains? I live at the top of a hill," and she shrugged, dismissing him already.

"People come by and peer in."

"Like you?"

The priest's pale face flushed bright scarlet. "I didn't know if anyone was home."

"So you thought you'd just peer in?" said Marguerite sounding bored with him.

"If you had curtains," said Father Aucoin, beginning to see a way to approach the matter, "I couldn't have looked in."

"Well, I'm not getting them," said Marguerite. "I don't like them. They make me feel closed in."

"But sometimes little boys come by," said Father Aucoin, feeling his stomach tighten and his face frown.

And then Marguerite Poirier exploded. "Why do you come up here to bother me? Do I come down to your church? Do I complain about certain priests who come here? Yes!" she said triumphantly. "Priests! And they don't want to just peer in the window, believe me. They want what's under my dress." And she made a strong, clear thrust with her hand toward the cleft between her thighs. "Do I come running to you with my problems? No, I leave you alone. I take care of my own problems and I'll thank you to leave it that way. Now get out of here and don't come back again, unless you want the same thing that Father Rory is so anxious for."

"I know about Father Rory," said Father Aucoin, feeling the constriction in his chest tighten further. "I hear his confession."

For a few moments, Father Aucoin looked very bleak and very young and it struck Marguerite Poirier with surprise that the priest was not much older than she, not more than thirty-five. A little on the thin side, she thought, nonetheless, a good-looking man, with flaxen hair, and large, brown eyes that opened onto the world wide, instead of squinting like a fisherman's.

Marguerite turned her back on him to put wood in the stove. She had a shapely back, broad at the shoulder and narrow at the waist before flaring out.

Father Simon turned and almost ran out of Marguerite Poirier's little house into the cut of the winter wind. He could not stay because he did not know what else to say or do. He was not used to opposition. It confused him. He was sweating. Sweating all along the back of his undershirt. He pushed the door shut behind him and the February cold mauled at him. The baking bread heat of Marguerite Poirier's kitchen evaporating towards the bleak stars. She should put up curtains, it was not a big thing to ask. But he did not dare confront her again.

He walked as quickly as he could down the lane to the harbour, across the bridge and then up to the other side past the Co-op and the Post Office. From there, Marguerite Poirier's windows were just small, squares of yellow in the dark, but clear, clear as a beacon.

The Priest's Boy

The boy sat on his father's shoulders while his father and Philibert strode across the fields towards the Presbytery, singing. Daniel's father had a fine, strong tenor and Philibert was loud. From his father's shoulders, the boy could see all the way down the coast line to the spire of St. Pierre in Chéticamp. The church spire stuck up like a pencil against the sky. He could see the land curve in front of him past sand beaches and headlands all the way to St. Joseph de la Mer.

He turned to get one last glimpse of the house, but it had already disappeared behind a little fold of land, and all he could see were fields and the mountains. He counted the fields between his house and the Presbytery. He decided that there weren't that many, but it seemed far because he could not see the house. His brothers would be in the barn now doing the evening milking. He would be filling the wood box for the kitchen stove, except he was not. He was going to the Presbytery, just like his brother Robert had done. He was going to be *le domestique de la prêtre*, the priest's boy. *Le domestique de la prêtre* flowed back and forth in his head. The words did not make much sense. He did not understand why the priest could not be married, and have his own sons to fill the wood box. Why should it have to be him? Every time he thought of this, it made him feel angry.

They arrived at the main road, swung along it, and then up the gravel path to the Presbytery. His father set him down on the porch, and then knocked at the door. Both his father and Philibert seemed to diminish as they walked in the front door. They were no longer princes. They held their caps in their hands. They were just Philibert, the matchmaker and Marcel Boudreau, the widower from Plateau.

Mrs. Cross, the housekeeper showed Daniel to his room. He had a whole room to himself. He set his clothes in one drawer of the chest. He wondered who would have enough clothes to fill up all these drawers. From his window, he could see the side of the church and part of the road. At home, he saw nothing but the mountains.

His father appeared in the doorway. "It looks comfortable, Daniel."

The boy said gravely, "It is all my own."

"I said that you would get a room to yourself. You never believe me."

His father came over and sat down on the bed, testing it. "Very comfortable, see it has good springs."

There was a silence.

"You will have fresh tea here, too, Daniel. Fresh tea and gingerbread cookies."

"Yes, Father."

"Robert was frightened at first too. But you'll get used to it. You'll be able to play the piano any time that you wish."

The boy looked so still and small, standing beside the bed, with one hand on the mattress and the other hanging down by his side that for a moment the father's resolution weakened. Perhaps, it would be better next year when he was older; yes, that would be better, but then next year the position might not be here.

He knelt down beside the boy and pulled him gently towards him into his arms.

"Daniel you are a lucky boy, you know that, don't you? Half the mothers in the parish are angry at me, because they wanted their own sons here, and we've already had one."

The boy nodded. He had heard it all before.

"You will be Father Aucoin's head altar boy. The other altar boys will look up to you. Father Aucoin will help you with your school work, just like he helped Robert. He will teach you how to play the piano."

He could feel the boy's heart beating wildly against his own.

"Look at where Robert is now, Daniel — on a scholarship. He's going to do well. Everybody knows that. I can't give you these things, Daniel. At home, you'd still have to bring in the wood. You'd still have to clean the cold ashes from the stove. You'd have just as many chores to do, but none of the advantages."

Marcel Boudreau sat his youngest son down on the edge of the bed and tried to ignore how he looked like his mother. How his hair was glossy and dark like hers with the same pale, fine skin and wide blue eyes.

"Your mother would want you to be here, Daniel. That's why I'm doing it. She would be angry if I let this chance slip by."

The boy nodded.

"You will be good, and make me proud of you. I know you will, just like Robert."

"I will be good," said the boy.

Marcel Boudreau sighed. It was not exactly the answer he wanted.

The sound of the piano began to come up the staircase. It was a crisp, clear sound unlike the great blur of chords that bellowed from the church organ. At the sound, Marcel could feel his son sit up beside him. He picked the boy up and carried him downstairs on his arm. He did not know why he did so, except he was used to carrying his youngest. He had gotten into the habit after Marie had died. It had comforted both of them.

Father Aucoin was sitting at the piano absorbed in the music, his hands flying quickly over the keys. The expression on his face intent, he paid them no attention. A little girl was sitting beside him, one of Theo Cormier's girls.

The smell of gingerbread cooking made its sweet way into the parlour. Mrs. Cross appeared at the parlour door wearing a long, white apron, her hands on her hips. Marcel Boudreau felt himself relax for the first time since he had left home with the boy.

"You see what I mean, Elodie?" said the priest, oblivious to anyone else. "Half of the music is the progression of the notes, the other half is the rhythm. You have to know which note follows which, yes, but you also have to know how they all fit together, that's called the rhythm. You can't have one without the other. When you go home, think of the rhythm of the piece, and try and tap it out with a fork, like this," and the priest began to tap on the edge of the piano with his fingertips. "Understand?"

Elodie Cormier nodded.

"Now, go get some cookies from Mrs. Cross."

The girl slipped off the bench and disappeared without a sound in the direction of the kitchen. The priest turned towards them. "And how are you, Daniel? Philibert tells me you can play the piano even better than your brother. Come, sit down beside me. We'll soon find out."

He opened the book. "Pick any tune you wish."

"He can't read music, but he knows where the notes are," said Marcel Boudreau intervening on behalf of his son. "If you play something, he can figure out how to play it by ear."

The priest bowed his head slightly in direction of Marcel Boudreau. "That is a talent. Let's see...try this," and he picked out a child's tune.

The boy immediately copied it note for note.

"And this."

This time the tune was harder. The boy hesitated for a minute as if he was doing addition in his head and then quickly copied the sound perfectly.

"Very good, and this?"

Again the boy hesitated for a minute, then copied the sound. This time he stumbled, for the piece was from the Mozart repertoire, and he had never heard anything like it before.

"I'm impressed," said the priest. "For once, my reprobate cousin does not seem to have exaggerated. You have a strong talent, young man, but we shall have to teach you a little about notes; you cannot hold everything in your head." He tapped the boy gently on the head. "There's too many notes, and not enough head, that's the problem."

The boy nodded, his blue eyes wide.

"Have you met Elodie Cormier?"

The boy shook his head.

"Well, she is a little younger than you, and she can read this without any trouble at all." The priest opened one of the books leaning against the piano. It showed a mass of black marks that looked like someone had thrown ink all over the page. The boy swallowed. It looked impossible. He could not imagine what all those black marks might mean.

"Could Robert read that?" he asked, wondering.

"Yes."

"Then, I have a long way to go to catch up to him," said Daniel, thinking about his brother.

"Yes, you do, but for now I would worry more about catching up to Elodie Cormier. She's more your age, and right now she is in the kitchen eating Mrs. Cross's gingerbread. You might see if you can catch up to her in gingerbread first, then we'll worry about music." The priest smiled, lines crinkling around his eyes. He looked years younger when he smiled.

The boy turned towards his father and his father pointed towards the kitchen. He needed no further encouragement. He swung his feet off the bench and followed Elodie into the kitchen.

Alone with the priest, Marcel Boudreau immediately felt the weight of his own inadequacies. He wished Philibert had stayed. Philibert knew how to deal with his cousin. He was able to say what he wanted without worrying about offending the priest or appearing stupid. Marcel Boudreau was mortally afraid of seeming stupid in front of the priest. He was not an educated man. He knew his letters, but reading was an effort. He preferred that Philibert read to him. It was so much faster. He could play the fiddle by ear, and that was about it. He had no other accomplishments. His life had mostly been chores. He had begun helping his father about the farm almost as soon as he could remember. He scarcely remembered going to school. In his day, only girls, and the weak boys went to school. He and Marie were married at nineteen. In spite of all his work, he had not been able to give her much ease. They had started having babies right away. They had been like two horses harnessed to the same plough.

The priest belonged to a different world. He had been to university. He did not lie in bed dreaming of the curve of a woman's body, the touch of her skin. The priest read prayers from his breviary. He taught children Latin and English and music. He went to parish meetings.

Marcel Boudreau could feel the parlour closing in on him. It felt complicated, intimidating. He did not see that the Presbytery parlour was furnished with thread-bare rugs and rough, wooden bookcases; that the piano was battered; that the books in the bookcases were second-hand editions with worn covers. To Marcel Boudreau, the Presbytery looked immensely rich, and filled with unattainable mysteries. Mysteries that his son Daniel could learn, but he could not.

He wanted to explain to the priest that Daniel was different from Robert, more fragile, that he should not expect Daniel to be like Robert. He thought Daniel was brighter. Brighter in every way, but he did not know how to say this to the priest without sounding stupid, without sounding as if he was a doting father preferring one child against another. Above all, he wanted to warn him to be careful with his youngest son. Instead, he thanked the priest for taking his son, shook his hand, and left quietly so that his son would not remark on his going.

His last image of Daniel was him sitting at the kitchen table with Elodie Cormier. Two glasses of milk and a large plate of cookies separated the blonde curls of Elodie and the dark head of Daniel.

The father did not see the boy look up as the priest opened the door for him, and in his eyes all the panic in the world was there.

Reds and Blues

Everybody knows the colour of hell is blue,
that's why Albert à Didier is so comfortable,
he's already there.

The sins that were laid at the door of Albert à Didier were so immense that they would have cracked the roof of heaven. He was a liar, a bully, a drinker, an impenitent womaniser and he did not take Communion. Worst of all, he was a Blue. Blue was the colour of greed, of scoundrels, the Conservative Party of Canada, and Albert à Didier.

Nowhere were two men more different than Albert à Didier and Simon Aucoin. Albert à Didier was a giant with a split veined face, a shock of dark hair, a beer hall voice who regarded Sunday as the day the bar closed in his hotel. Simon Aucoin was a thin, fair man who still had the air of a choir boy about him. He did not drink; supported the Credit Union and followed the Bishop's instructions that he was to encourage the spiritual growth of St. Joseph de la Mer. It was also known, he was Red. Red was the colour of the Liberal Party of Canada.

Before each election Albert à Didier would take his boat, La Chanceux, to St. Pierre et Miquelon and return with barrels of rum. These would be hidden away until a few days before the election, to be brought at the last minute to convince the confused that Blue was indeed a celestial colour. It was as bad or as good as La Chandeleur. Men would roll home drunk and the women would stay away from them until the election was over and the rum from St. Pierre had dried up.

Father Aucoin did not like drinking at any time for any reason and he had preached against alcohol many times, but he had never preached against Albert à Didier. It was one thing to preach against some poor lumberjack who came out of the bush, got soused and then beat up someone in a drunken fit; that was expected. Lumberjacks always got drunk. It was part of their nature and it was part of Father

Aucoin's nature to preach against them. But preaching against Albert à Didier, 'l'homme fort du French shore' was another thing entirely. He had friends in high places. He was not predictable. He had a tendency to lose his temper like a cranky bear and when he did nothing was sacred, not even the church.

Nonetheless, Father Aucoin decided it was not right that votes should be bought with booze and one Sunday, a month or so before the election he preached against it. He mentioned no names. He did not even use the word rum. He did not say who to vote for, he only said that a vote was a vote and it should not be for sale at any price. Selling your vote was wrong and he went on for some time in this way, using as he usually did illustrations from the Bible. It was a jubilant day for the Reds in the village and it downcast all the Blues as they took it to mean that Father Simon was supporting the Liberal Party of Canada.

When Albert à Didier heard what had happened, his jaw fell open, his face contorted, and he let out a bellow that could be heard from one end of the harbour to the other. "That damn' priest! That God damn' priest! He can keep his God damn' opinions to himself!" Albert à Didier bellowed one curse after another all the way up to the Presbytery. They preceded him like an advancing wave and he surfed in behind them like some wrathful pagan God determined to slay the Christian usurper. He barged right into the Presbytery kitchen. His big hand came up. He shook his forefinger under the nose of Father Aucoin and told him then and there if he didn't eat his words and eat them from the pulpit, he'd make damn' sure the Bishop found him a new parish to preach in, "somewhere east of Skir Dhu." And then he vanished back to his car and back to the harbour where he was preparing La Chanceux to sail for St. Pierre.

Now, there were many things which did not terrify Father Aucoin. To death and injury, he was impervious, but the thought of losing his parish which was dearer to him than life itself, was terrifying. Albert à Didier had cleverly touched the one *point faible* in the terrestrial armour of Father Aucoin.

The same awful thought kept running through the mind of Father Simon. The Bishop was a Blue. A Tory right down to his episcopal socks and it was a great aggravation to him that so many of his younger clergy were Red. He had sent out Diocesian epistles which warned against the dangers of the social gospel; which reminded his priests that they were in their parishes to be spiritual leaders, not Credit Union managers.

In brief, the Bishop, who, like Albert à Didier was a bulky man inclined to fortified wines and a sharp temper, did not like his clergy messing about with anything that smacked of politics, unless it had a Blue tinge. He had exiled Father Jimmy Tomkins to Wreck Cove for organising a Fisherman's Co-op, and Father Simon had no doubt the same thing could happen to him. Albert à Didier's arm was long. Albert à Didier insolently continued to prepare La Chanceux to sail for St. Pierre leaving Father Aucoin to ponder his dilemma, and ponder he did. He had, after all, chosen his words very carefully. He had said nothing about Parties, nothing about voting Conservative or Liberal. He had carefully steered clear of politics. He had said simply that one should vote according to conscience, not rum. But then, Jimmy Tomkins had done nothing wrong either, but his Guysborough Fishing Co-op had displaced a businessman by the name of John Donald Campbell. If that was enough to get Jimmy Tomkins sent to Wreck Cove, then as sure as eggs were eggs and Albert à Didier was a Blue, he was headed for Skir Dhu.

Father Aucoin grew moody and withdrawn. His halo slipped. He snapped at the altar boys and growled at his housekeeper. He spent a good deal of time on his prie dieu, but the prayers did not help. All week long, he felt Albert à Didier's words clawing in his belly. His nightmare would come true. The Bishop would call him down to Antigonish. There would be a frosty interview. The Bishop would look over his reading glasses and say "Simon, I see you've been in St. Joseph de la Mer for almost eighteen years, that's a long time. Time for a change, don't you think?"

It would do no good to protest for the harder he protested, the more it would look like he was a Red. All week long, Father Simon mulled this over. One minute determined to stand up for what he believed in, he would not be bullied by Albert à Didier. If he was, he might as well accept free rum for his vote. The next, he was chastened and apologetic. Perhaps, there had been a misunderstanding. Perhaps, he had not chosen his words carefully enough. The week took forever.

On Sunday, the church was crammed from the balcony to the altar rail. The Reds led by William Doucet, were sure that Father Aucoin could not be bullied. The Blues led by Albert à Didier, were sure that he could.

The Mass began in a kind of haze for Father Simon. He seemed to have trouble seeing and hearing. The familiar words floated from his mouth as if from someone else. Everything seemed at a distance, until he climbed up to the pulpit. Then the morning began to come into focus and he could see and hear his congregation. The young men seated along the first rail of the balcony so that they could see the girls down below. The choir clustered around the organ. Then his eyes swept along the main floor of his little church. There was Gerard à Levis seated at the back, his arms folded comfortably across his chest, his head already lolling. It was well-known that the only place that Gerard à Levis ever got a decent sleep was at Mass. Rosaries began to clack and children to shuffle, his congregation was beginning to fret. They wanted to hear him speak clearly with no apology in his voice.

Father Aucoin took a deep breath and looked straight at Albert à Didier. He said his words clearly so there could be no misunderstanding. He apologised for mixing in the affairs of Caesar as he had done last Sunday. His homily was full of learned references to St. Paul, but there was no mistaking the smile on the face of Albert à Didier as he listened to Big Shot, Father Aucoin, eat crow in his own Church.

Moving Ice

I will avoid the occasion for sin.
I will not look at girls.
I will avoid the occasion for sin.
I will not look at girls.

The boy scrawled in a brown paper scribbler at the kitchen table. It was the kind of scribbler where the paper is so rough that you can still find bits of wood chips flattened like moles on the pages. If he pressed too hard, the point of the pencil tore the paper and if he did not press hard enough the words were so faint that they were difficult to read. Every time he finished a line, he looked up from the table to see if the lights in the church had been switched off. They remained bright rectangles of light.

Without closing his eyes, he could see Father Aucoin kneeling at one of the pews, his hands clasped in front of himself, praying. The boy imagined a river of prayers flowing out of Father Aucoin through the windows of the church towards heaven. Before he came down to breakfast, the priest prayed at a little prie dieu in his bedroom. There was mass at seven, the Angelus at noon. When he walked about the parish, he carried his breviary and read from it when he stopped to rest.

The boy pushed his pencil across the paper. *I will avoid the occasion for sin. I will not look at girls.* And he wrote a tiny 56 in the margin to indicate exactly where he was. Writing the numbers down wouldn't help him to get to 100 any faster, but he could not seem to help it. Fifty-six felt more solid than forty-six, safer. He was getting somewhere.

Everything for Father Aucoin was the occasion for sin. Swimming offered the occasion for sin. Square dancing offered the occasion for sin. Pocket watches offered the occasion for sin. The little injuries floated up in Daniel Boudreau's soul like the weeds that he pulled from the presbytery garden. Bitter and prickly, they peppered the space in front of his eyes until he could not write any longer.

What good did praying do anyway?

He had prayed for his mother every night, kneeling by the edge of his bed until his knees were sore and his back stiff. He had prayed to be allowed to stay home, instead his father had sent him to the Presbytery. "It will be good for you. The tea is fresh," said his father. Not a word about avoiding the occasion for sin. "The tea is fresh."

At home, they had said grace before meals and a prayer before bed. On Sunday, like everyone else, they went to Mass. His mother had trimmed his hair when he had been chosen to be an altar boy. But he never got the impression that his mother thought a great deal about praying. It was just something that you did like brushing your teeth.

It was only when she began to cough that the boy began to think about praying. How many prayers equalled one cough. One night when his mother was coughing, coughing in the room behind the kitchen stove, he decided that he would make a deal with God. For every Hail Mary that he said his mother would have one cough less. He stuck his hand up open towards the ceiling and shook hands with God. Each night the boy prayed fiercely until his throat was dry and raw from saying the words.

Not long after he had arrived at the Presbytery, when they were sitting down to supper, he decided to ask the priest what he prayed for.

Father Aucoin squinted into the light of the kerosene lamp, thought for a moment and said, "different things."

"You pray to move the ice off the lobster grounds, don't you?"

"Did Peter à Peter tell you that?"

"Yes."

Father Aucoin stopped eating his breakfast off towards the window. "Each spring the fishermen ask me to pray for the ice to move off the lobster grounds," he said, shrugging his thin shoulders. "It is not something I choose."

"How does a prayer work to push ice? Is it like a big hand that just comes down and pushes the ice along?" the boy asked, trying to imagine 'Our father who art in heaven,' pushing along a great field of ice.

Father Aucoin pressed his lips into a thin line against his teeth. It was a sign the boy would learn to beware.

"No, I don't think so."

"Then how does it work?" persisted the boy because he thought that surely the priest must know.

"I'm not sure," he said finally. He tapped the heel of his fork lightly against the table. "What about you, young man, what do you pray for?"

"I pray for a pocket watch. I would like a pocket watch like my father's. Then I would be able to know exactly what time it was when I woke in the morning."

"How much does a pocket watch cost?"

"A dollar," the boy replied quickly, because he had examined it often enough at the Co-op.

"A dollar is a lot of money," said Father Aucoin, shaking his head sadly as if this was as difficult to attain as moving ice.

I will not look at girls. I will avoid the occasion for sin. The boy marked 71 neatly beside the last word. Then he put his pencil down and began to rub his fingers which were cramping. He stood up from the table, stretched and went to the piano where he began to fiddle with the keys.

He had lied although he did not think of it as lying. He had said it automatically. He had wanted a pocket watch and the priest expected him to be praying for something, so he had said pocket watch. He was not conscious of lying, but the truth was he had given up praying for anything.

At the presbytery, he had quickly learned to avoid the occasion for prayer. At bedtime, he pretended to be asleep in his bed so that he would miss evening prayers and during Mass, the boy prayed with such practised efficiency that he scarcely knew what he was saying. He drifted through Mass from the *Confiteor* to the Postcommunion in perfect time without pausing, without hesitation, rarely missing a beat. The Mass was like an old tune which he could play in his sleep.

"I confess to Almighty God, to blessed Mary, ever virgin, to blessed Michael the Archangel, to blessed John the Baptist, the holy Apostles, Peter and Paul, and to you, Father, that I have sinned exceedingly in thought, word and deed, through my fault, through my fault, through my most grievous fault."

He phrased the response just right. Letting his voice build in a natural, musical climax towards 'grievous,' which rang like a bell when he said it and then resolved perfectly into 'fault.' The other boys followed Daniel's voice.

Elodie Cormier sat in the fifth row from the altar rail. She was not from the improving side of the parish. Her father was not a pillar of the community. He had a small holding on which he kept a few cows, pigs and chickens, but he was not much of a farmer. Theo Cormier mostly specialised in getting by. He avoided contact with anyone who showed signs of wanting 'to improve him.' This included his wife, his daughters and Father Aucoin. Theo Cormier wasn't exactly a sinner, but neither was he interested in applying for sainthood. Left to his own devices, he liked to sit on an overturned barrel, roll cigarettes, and talk. Theo had seven daughters, one for each day of the week, he liked to say.

The boy did not pray for anything, but he did save money for a pocket watch. After Mass, the priest gave each one of his altar boys a five cent piece. As soon as Daniel had saved a dollar, he went to the Co-op and bought himself a pocket watch. It was the first thing that he had ever bought in the Co-op store. He kept it under his mattress at night and during the day in his front pocket tied with a string to his belt exactly the way that his father did.

The priest did not notice the new watch which was amazing because the boy consulted it at every opportunity, mostly to see if it was still working for he had a terror that it might stop.

When the priest did notice, he immediately flew into a great temper. How could the boy be so unthinking as to waste a dollar on a pocket watch? How stupid could he be? A dollar could be spent in so many wiser ways. There was his schooling to think about. There was....On and on, until the great joy of the new pocket watch was entirely spoiled.

I will not look at girls, the boy wrote carefully. What was he supposed to do, then? Look heavenwards? He had fallen in love. He had not expected it. For the longest time, he was not even conscious of Elodie. She was just one of Theo Cormier's daughters. He saw her every Sunday in an absent-minded sort of way. It was his father and older brothers that he liked to watch, for they always participated in the liturgy with clear, robust voices. The Boudreaus may have been poor, but they had fine voices, and he would be filled with pride when he heard them.

Theo Cormier's daughters sat on the other side of the church from the Boudreaus and the boy began to find staring at them to be the most pleasant thing in the world. For the longest time, he could not make up his mind which one he liked best until like a gate coming down inside him, he discovered it was Elodie. It was to Elodie his eyes kept returning. Elodie had blonde hair, blue eyes and a pale, clear complexion. When the sunlight came through the side windows and fell upon Elodie as she bent her head a halo seemed to dance about her. There were moments when the boy would not have been surprised if Elodie Cormier had sprouted wings and begun to fly heavenwards.

The boy's fingers tore up the scales. He could play scales faster than Father Aucoin. It was the only thing that he could do better than the priest and he enjoyed it. His fingers were more nimble. "Rhythm, Daniel, remember the rhythm. You're not racing a car. Music doesn't mean anything without rhythm," the priest would call from another part of the house as soon as he heard Daniel attacking the piano. Then he would come and stand at the piano until the boy had slowed down. It was the one sure way he had of annoying Father Aucoin. The boy ripped up and down the scales for a long time, forgetting that the priest was still in the church and he was annoying no one.

He went back to the kitchen table and began writing once more.

I will not look at girls.

I will avoid the occasion for sin.

The boy pencilled in 80 at the end of "sin." The desire to rip the pages into little pieces swept over him. Rip, rip, rip into little squares. He sat on his hands and waited for the feeling to pass.

Elodie's father was not a pillar of the community, that was the problem. He came to church, but mostly to talk before and after Mass. He paid little attention to the liturgy. He belonged to no improving societies. He was not a member of the Credit Union. He came to no study groups. Theo Cormier was an occasion for sin, therefore his daughters must be also. It had taken the boy a long time to figure this out, but once he had he was sure of it.

His own father was not a pillar of the community either. He could not earn much money. He remembered that the year his mother had died, his father had managed to earn thirty-three dollars. "Thirty-three dollars!" he remembered his father's astonished voice telling the story to Philibert, the Matchmaker. It seemed like a lot of money to Daniel. His father laughed when he heard this and sat him down on his knee. The Boudreaus had not been lucky, but he was lucky to be taken in by Father Aucoin. Philibert and his father had explained this to him.

They explained that Father Aucoin had a piano; that the priest would teach him to play. He was musical like his mother. Father Aucoin was an educated man. All the boys who stayed at the presbytery did well. It was a great chance for him. The boy did not know how to tell his father that he did not want to go. He was ten. His father packed his bag and swung him up on his shoulders before they were even out of the house.

Philibert and his father were big, strong men and they came strolling across the fields towards the church, his father and Philibert singing, his father in tune, Philibert in an off key. But they sounded fin, happy, full of life. It had seemed like a grand arrival as if he was a prince.

Mrs. Cross, the housekeeper opened the door and Philibert set him down on the porch. Father Aucoin appeared. He was dressed in his soutane, a long, thin streak of black at the door. His blonde hair and pale face accentuated by the dark soutane. Philibert and his father doffed their caps when the priest arrived and took their boots off at the Presbytery door. They seemed to be dissolving in front of the boy's eyes. When they sat down for tea in the kitchen, he noticed that his father's trousers were patched and the sleeves of his shirt were ragged. He'd never noticed this before, but he did now and he thought of what his father had said: the Boudreaus were not lucky.

Mrs. Cross showed him the chores. He must stoke the furnace before he went to bed, that was his chore. He must clean the stables before he went to bed, that was his chore. He must clean the stables before Mrs. Cross went to milk and put fresh hay in the mangers. Mrs. Cross washed up in the morning, but he washed up in the evening. After breakfast, he served early morning mass with Father Aucoin, then he went to school.

He had a bedroom all to himself. Through the window, he could see the side of the church which in the moonlight seemed like the side of a great, white ship, but the ship was stuck, it wasn't moving. He wanted to go home. He wanted his mother back and he went to the window. There was nothing to see but stars. It felt as if the stars were getting smaller and smaller, and he was falling into a deep, dark hole.

I will not look at girls.
I will avoid the occasion for sin.

The boy marked 90 down beside "sin." The lights went off in the church. The boy felt a rush of panic. He had not finished yet. He was still short of a hundred. He bent his head down and tried to write more quickly. The tip of the pencil tore the paper. He sat on his hands and counted to ten to calm himself. When Father Aucoin entered the kitchen, he was finishing his ninety-first line.

The priest ran his finger down the neat rows of line and said "I hope you've learned your lesson, Daniel."

The boy said "Yes."

"Very well, you can go to bed now."

The boy went to bed and dreamed of Elodie Cormier. One day, he would run away. He would run away to some place far.

On Sunday, the fishermen asked Father Aucoin if he would pray to keep the ice off the lobster grounds, but the priest said he could not do it anymore. He said it was too hard.

Philibert Confesses

"In the name of the Father, Son
and Holy Ghost. Bless me Father,
for I have sinned. It has been one
year since I have been to confession."

The first time that I saw her it did not surprise me that she did not have a husband. She dressed like a man, braces, rough work shirts, wool trousers, her hair tied up in a bun at the back. I remember thinking to myself what a strange incarnation. But she was a woman and once the first shock of the attire left, you could tell that easily enough.

I wrote a letter for the old man. I listened to the gossip and all the time from the corner of my eye I watched her. She knew this, but it did not seem to bother her. She seemed if anything completely indifferent to me. She helped her mother clean up always with the same profound expression, as if she was in love, but her lover was at a great, great distance from her. But who would love this woman? She was the youngest daughter and far beyond the normal time of marriage. I guessed her to be twenty-six or twenty-seven.

Normally, it is not difficult to find a woman a husband, a husband a wife. Names always pop into my mind. I can't help it. Sylvie and Armand, Elodie and Joseph, Michele and Denis, the names roll so quickly together that I cannot stop them. And then I start comparing them. Elodie is beautiful. She plays the piano. She sings, but she would drive Joseph, who is a quiet, modest boy, crazy and I cross Elodie off from Joseph. Instead I try her out with Denis, who is a hard driving, impatient man who would not worry one shit if his wife wore her opinions on his back. If she yelled at him, he'd yell right back. Yes, Elodie and Denis, they go well together.

You see, Father, the great trick is not to find the woman and the man, the trick is to find the right man for the right woman. One that will not grind on the other, that is the great difficulty. I wish that I had had a matchmaker when I got married. Someone to take me aside and say, see, this is the woman for you. She is just right. Trust me. Instead like all young fools, I jumped into the first warm bed I found.

Anyway, I left the house of the sad-faced young woman, and not one name popped into my head. No Denis or Armand, not a one came to mind. Young men did not want a woman who could swing an axe better than they, and older men want someone to keep them thinking they are young. Someone who has learned to laugh at all the nonsense that presents itself as life.

I began to visit more often. Sometimes, I would see her. Sometimes I would not. She worked with her father a good deal. She had a wonderful smile. It came as such a surprise.

In one instant, she would change from this dour, poetic expression to great joy. I never got tired of seeing her smile and I began to contrive ways of making her smile, a funny story, a little present. She smiled easily enough, more easily than many women.

One day I asked her why she had such a sad expression and she just shrugged and said, it was like that. Her mother overheard me and she began to pester the girl. How was she going to get a husband when she looked like her mother had just died. Why couldn't she smile more? She looked fine when she smiled. And on and on. The girl ran away to work in the barn and then the mother continued right on at me until I went out to the barn also.

As soon as she saw me, she raised her hands to the sky and said, "Am I supposed to walk around grinning like a fool? Is that what makes men happy? Fools?"

"No," I replied. "But you could dress up more. You look like a ragmuffin."

"I work with my father. What am I supposed to do, dress in a skirt to shovel manure and chase cows?"

"No, that makes no sense, but you are beautiful and it is hard to see. You seem to hide behind ugly clothes."

She smiled when I said this and I grew confused and left. It was as if she had kissed me. I felt both elated and terrified.

After that the girl and I often talked, but it was as if there was a barrier between us. I would say a few words. She would say a few words. We were like two people with a terrible stutter, because I could not really say what was on my mind and nor could she.

One day, I was coming home from Cheticamp and my old horse was tired, so I took a detour up to the little pond hidden behind the Aucoin's farm. I thought to rest there as I had done when I was a boy. The pond was just as I remembered it, still and perfect. I unhitched the horse and took my shoes off. There was a boy swimming about in the middle of the lake diving this way and that like an otter.

It was hot and I decided that I was not too old to swim either. I stripped my clothes off and dove into the water. It was cool, crystals of delight as wonderful to the skin as I remembered and I began to forget that I had passed my fortieth year. I began to think that I was just starting out. I waved to the boy, but he began to swim at a terrific pace towards the shore, faster than I have ever seen anyone swim.

It was the girl. When she drew herself up on the shore, she stood there for a long moment looking directly at me. She was naked as the day she was born and more beautiful than I had ever imagined, slim-hipped, tall, graceful. If she had had a bow and arrow in her hands, she could have shot me dead in the water, so transfixed was I, and then she disappeared into the woods.

I swam slowly back to the shore in a terrible state of mind. I was in love that was clear enough, but I was also married with children. What should I do? What should I do? I decided for once in my life I would be bold. I would drive straight to her house. I would explain that I loved her sad face, her beautiful smile, her modesty, her way of being unto herself. We would run away to Boston together.

The wheel fell off my buggy and I could not find the pin which had held it. I had to walk all the way to Gerard à Levis. Every time I put the wheel back on, it would turn for a few turns and then start to come off again. By the time that I got to Gerard à Levis, I was sweating in a fury of frustration. Worse, he was shoeing a cranky horse and would pay no attention to me, not a minute, so I was obliged to search for a cotter pin myself among his odds and ends and finished by cutting my hand on some steel. Not until I had bled over everything in sight would Gerard à Levis come and help me. Then he fixed the wheel in an instant.

My hand would not stop bleeding and I was obliged to go to the house where Gerard's wife cleaned and bound it. I drove by my own house and then went by the back road up to the LeVerts. By the hill paths, it is only about twenty minutes from the Aucoin's pond to the LeVerts. But what with the broken cotter pin, the cut hand and the road, it had taken me about three hours. I arrived with my hair matted, out of breath, blood on the front of my shirt, looking like a wild man. The LeVerts were sitting at the kitchen table eating supper. There was a young man with them that I had never seen before sitting opposite Julie. Her hair was let down and it hung in thick, auburn ringlets to her shoulders. I had never seen anyone but old people at the LeVerts before. I had never seen Julie's hair let down before. I was so astonished by all this that I bolted like a frightened rabbit with my heart thundering in my ears.

I went back the next day and apologised for bursting in on their dinner. I made a lame excuse. Julie walked with me to my horse. We stood for a few seconds in silence together. I cold not go on like this anymore. I told her the real reason for my visit; that I had seen her at the pond; that I loved her. She said it was all right because she loved me also.

The young man is a cousin from Margaree who had come to help the family with the hay.

So that is the long and the short of it, Father. Now, I must go home and tell my wife and children. When I left the LeVerts I fully intended to do it, but there must be some kind of block inside me. I see my house, think of my children and everything freezes. I do not understand why. My wife is happiest when I'm not bothering her. She is very independent. She doesn't much like a man around the house. She likes to be left alone to do exactly as she pleases. What is wrong with me? Am I sick?

"You are a good man, Philibert."

"But I don't want to be a good man. I want to be like Albert à Didier."

"Albert à Didier is a sinner."

"Perhaps, but what is the point of being a good man? Good men confuse virtue and common sense. I will never find another girl like this and she will never find someone who can make her smile like I can. She'll marry some oaf who treats her like her family does, like a prize cow that must be kept in braces and work clothes, and I will spend the rest of my days being that odd character, the matchmaker with the cranky wife. What good is there to that?"

"You have done the right thing, Philibert. For your impure thoughts, say five Hail Marys and two Our Fathers at each station of the cross, and avoid the occasion for sin; stay away from Julie LeVert."

La Chandeleur de Dulcine

It's Monsieur, the husband and Madame, the wife.
It's Monsieur, the husband and Madame, the wife.
They haven't yet had any supper.
A small mill by the river,
A small mill to power with water.
There's a fire on the mountain, run boy run.
There's a fire on the mountain, run boy run.
I've seen the wolf, the fox, the hare.
I've seen the great, city jump.
I've stepped on my green blanket.
I've stepped on my green blanket with my feet.
Aouenne, aoenn', genille.
Ah! recou' ta genille.
Aouenne, aouenne, aouenne, nippaillon!

L'escauouette,
Song of the chandeleur

Dulcine Leblanc was the youngest daughter of a sea captain who had once been an important figure in the village. He had owned a large house not far from the church with a splendid view of the farms which rolled away down the little valley of the Moine. But he had lost his boat in a storm, it was not insured and the bank took everything. The Captain was forced to move to a little cabin down by the harbour that he had once used to shelter his nets and dry goods. It was a long way to the church from the harbour and the Captain was too old and proud to ask for a ride, so he and his family stopped coming to Mass.

Hector Leblanc was already an old man when all this happened. He did not have the energy or the money to start over. He spent his time quietly by the harbour talking with other old men about the days of sail. His youngest child, Dulcine, grew up without the church, without school, in the most terrible poverty. She would scavenge along the beach for coloured stones in front of her little cabin and pretend the stones were toys. If one of her older brothers brought her a dollar when they visited, her mother would take it. From the youngest age, she took care of children for neighbours and in this way and that the family earned enough to feed themselves.

The people of St. Joseph de la Mer gradually forgot about the old Captain. They forgot that he had once lived in a grand house near the church and owned a schooner called the Hector Leblanc. They remembered only that he was poor and at Christmas time the Captain and his family would receive a large basket filled with food. Afterwards, it was said, William à Joseph Doucet first met Dulcine delivering Christmas baskets.

At the time of the Chandeleur, Dulcine would have been twenty or twenty-one. She was beautiful. There was no other way to describe her. Raven black hair, blue, blue eyes set in a fair face and no dress in the world could disguise her figure. She did not look like a witch. She looked like a princess. A princess born into the most terrible poverty.

The summer before Dulcine's Chandeleur, the nuns in Cheticamp took pity on her and gave her a small job making beds and cleaning the floors in the hospital. For the first time in her life, Dulcine had a little money and she saved enough to buy a dress for Sunday. She began to come to Mass. She came all by herself without either her mother or father. She walked the entire length of the parish, past the fish plant, past the Co-op store, past the Post Office, past the Credit Union, all the way down the sea front to the Presbytery and the Church of St. Joseph.

In church, Dulcine was like a wild thing that had wandered in the door. She could not follow the Mass from a book because she could not read. She had no rosary. She stared about her like a tourist, gaping at this, delighted at that; she did not know what anything meant. It was all interesting to her and she could see why people liked to go to Mass. It was a good show. Afterwards, Dulcine told Father Aucoin that she loved the music and asked if she could come again. The good priest was shocked and said "Of course, my child. Of course."

The curious thing was Dulcine Leblanc did not understand in the slightest way her effect on men. She looked like a Princess. A princess who knew as much about sin as a turtle. When Dulcine came to Mass, she made the women nervous and the men gathered around her like bees to clover. It was all mysterious to Dulcine. She gathered the stories of the men and played with them as she had with the coloured stones that she used to collect as a child on the beach. She did not imagine that men were faithful to wives or wives faithful to men. But then she did not imagine them to be unfaithful either. She did not imagine anything to be quite the way it was told to her.

Dulcine confused men with her bright laugh and her piercing blue eyes. They wanted to touch her, to feel the texture of her soft, dark hair against their skin, but Dulcine did not understand this craving either. She had lived too long alone with aged parents who had treated her with the distant affection of a favourite pet. Her mind was like a starving man's appetite. It roamed here and there, fastening onto this, letting go of that. She wanted desperately to be educated, to add and subtract the sums of the universe, to read about the woes of the world from the newspaper like the Matchmaker; above all, she wanted to feel that she occupied a space on the planet that was clearly marked Dulcine Leblanc. Instead, her mind wandered and when she looked at Dulcine Leblanc, she did not see a Princess with raven locks and regal bearing. She saw nothing much in particular, nothing more than an insubstantial outline in the shore mist.

The Chandeleur began with the women making the candles for the priest to bless. Once the candles were blessed, when one lit a Chandeleur candle, the small flame was supposed to calm a stormy night as if all the warmth and merriment of the Chandeleur was stored in the candles.

On the morning of the Chandeleur, three teams of men were chosen to drive timber sleighs from house to house to collect food for the party. For la chandeleur de Dulcine, the sleighs were led by a young farmer named William à Joseph Doucet. It was he who carried the Chandeleur cane decorated with bright ribbons.

At each house, he would sing a song, a nonsense song and at the end of the song, he would be given some food for the party. When they came to the harbour, they stopped at the blacksmith's, at the post office, at the Credit Union, and they stopped at the Captain's little shack. The young farmer was determined to leave no one out. William à Joseph and his friends sang their song and danced their dance, but as they had expected, the Captain's wife had no food for them. Dulcine was standing by the door watching them and the young farmer said, "We will take Dulcine with us. She will enjoy the day."

Before the old woman could say yea or nay, Dulcine had jumped onto the sleigh and hid herself under the buffalo robes. The young farmer clacked the reins and the horses jumped away. The harness bells jingling merrily and the bright winter sunlight turning the white snow to blue and white crystals of light.

It was the first time that Dulcine had been out and about in society by herself and it was all marvellous to her. With blue eyes wide as saucers, she watched the young farmer dance and sing on the porch of each farm house and then afterwards receive a pot of this or a plate of that. Sometimes, it was only a loaf of bread, but always William was given something. All this amazed Dulcine; she had never seen or heard so much jolly laughter. A halo seemed to surround the blonde head of the young farmer. Everywhere he went people liked and admired him. He would joke and laugh and he sang in a clear, musical tenor that was pleasing to hear. She watched him and wished, for the first time, that she had someone like him to keep her company.

***

At the Chandeleur, Dulcine listened to the table conversation like a child; laughing where she should not laugh, serious where she should be laughing. The women did not know what to make of her, no more did the men. She could not dance, although there were enough willing teachers. The moves defeated her. She did not like to drink. She mostly stood quietly and watched the dancers twirl about the kitchen.

Late in the evening, when the dancers grew tired, Linus P. Chiasson began to tell stories. He was the great story teller of St. Joseph de la Mer. His stories always began, "now that reminds me," and the people would grow quiet while Linus remembered a family of sorcerers or a man who came from Paris and drowned in the sea. Linus knew hundreds of stories. There was no one else like him on the French Shore.

Dulcine Leblanc listened enraptured, and the harder she listened, the more outrageous his stories became. Ugly mermaids transformed themselves into storms, storms into disconsolate young men, dogs into devils. There was nothing too amazing for Linus P. Chiasson to invent.

The young farmer who had brought Dulcine to the Chandeleur was a fine young dancer and all the ladies wanted to dance with him, but he would not dance. He spent his time at the side of Dulcine. When she listened to Linus tell stories, he listened. When she went to the kitchen to socialise, he went until the ladies gave up on him and went to look for other partners.

The Chandeleur ended Sunday morning the way it always did with Gerard à Levis trying to fly to the stars by jumping off the porch roof into a snow bank. And as the sun was just peeking over the edge of the sea a terrific fight broke out between Felix à Medric and Zacherie Cormier over something of great importance. Several other fights of lesser interest quickly broke out. When the sun was finally truly up, Gerard à Levis stopped trying to fly to the stars and was taken into the house to thaw out in front of the stove. Outside, there were enough bloody noses to keep everyone happy. It was time to go home. The horses were hitched up and it was noticed by a few that Dulcine Leblanc was driven home by the young farmer who was considered to be a pillar of the community. She rested her head on his shoulder which did not go unnoticed either.

Father Aucoin surveyed the ragged edges of his congregation with the usual despair of February second. The young men in the front row of the balcony looked like the remains of a war zone, so brightly did their bloodshot eyes shine. As usual, the married men with the black eyes and big heads were seated nodding quietly at the back, the henpecked and the virtuous ostentatiously at the front. It was the same way every February second and Father Aucoin vowed again that he would not bless the Chandeleur candles. From the pulpit, he gave the sinners a long and vehement harangue about the despair of sin and the glories of heaven which made the virtuous feel more virtuous and the sinners accomplished.

Now, it was one thing to be foolish at the Chandeleur, that was in a way permitted. People turned a blind eye, but it was entirely another thing to visit a young woman in broad daylight when one's own wife was sitting home eight months pregnant. "Entirely another thing!" sniffed the Postmistress to Genevieve who came to get her pension cheque at ten o'clock, who turned and sniffed to Sylvie her daughter, who told her best friend Marie Laure, who put her hands on her hips and said "damnation" with great authority, as she was a woman to whom authority came naturally. In this way, up and down the parish, without a telephone being lifted, every woman in St. Joseph de la Mer learned of the calumny of William à Joseph Doucet. Every woman that is except Margaret Doucet who was the wife of William à Joseph. Nobody thought to mention it to her.

Now, William à Joseph Doucet was a pillar of the community. A young man of impeccable character, who had raised himself by hard, hard work to own a large farm. It had been no accident that he had been chosen to lead the Chandeleur sleighs as the men knew this would find favour with their testy priest. For when Father Aucoin thought of the future of St. Joseph de la Mer, he often thought of William à Joseph. He was one of the men the priest depended upon to be steady and exemplary without being sententious. Thus while the women might cackle, the men kept their peace because William à Joseph was a handy man to know from both sides of the parish fence.

The young farmer himself appeared in no way guilty or discomforted. He just shrugged and said he went to listen to Dulcine tell stories. When Linus P. Chiasson heard this he laughed and quickly asked: "And when was the last time William à Joseph ever listened to any story but the song of his plough?" Pretty soon the whole village was laughing at the notion of the song of William's plough, which by all accounts was a fertile one.

Father Aucoin prayed.

Curious about all this, Linus P. Chiasson went round to visit Dulcine, and he found her in good spirits, no more bothered by all the gossip than William à Joseph. They had tea together in her ragged kitchen and Dulcine begged Linus to tell her a story. Not long after that, Margaret Doucet went to the hospital in Cheticamp to have her baby and she met Dulcine there. Dulcine had raised more babies than she could remember and the two women got to talking.

Margaret told Dulcine about living with a pillar of the community which seemed interesting to Dulcine, and Dulcine told Margaret about living down by the harbour, which seemed interesting to Margaret. Dulcine decided that living with a pillar of the community had its advantages and disadvantages and Margaret decided that she was glad her husband was not a fisherman and did not sleep away from home on long summer nights.

Just before Margaret was to come back to St. Joseph de la Mer, the baby became very sick. It coughed and cried, coughed and cried. When Margaret became too tired to hold the baby, Dulcine would hold the baby and in this way the two women rocked and bathed the fever away. To pass the time, Margaret began to teach Dulcine her letters. The long and the short of it was, they saved the baby's life and became friends.

When Margaret went home, Dulcine began to visit her at William à Josephs' and Margaret continued to teach Dulcine to read. It was a great revelation to Dulcine that it was such a simple thing to read. She had always thought reading was more mysterious than learning a, b, c. She was a bit disappointed although she did not tell

Margaret this. Dulcine learned so quickly that it was soon she who was reading to Margaret's children, although she found these "bought" stories tiresome and preferred to make up her own.

William à Joseph stopped visiting Dulcine.

To the chagrin of the postmistress, the scandal seemed to have resolved itself most unsatisfactorily, which is to say without her help. Dulcine was clearly not a good woman. It wasn't natural for a woman to be as beautiful as Dulcine and wear flowers in her hair. Clearly, she was a witch.

Father Aucoin could not make up his mind, either. Somehow, it did not seem right, but then, he did not know exactly what was wrong, either. Dulcine was clearly a good woman. The nuns had explained to him how she had stayed up night after night with Margaret Doucet's baby. But, she did not come to church often and when she did, there was something about Dulcine that disturbed him.

On Sunday, he watched William à Joseph carefully for any signs of changes, but the young man conducted himself as he always did with a kind of bright dignity that was neither fawning nor overly proud. And Father Aucoin reminded himself that William à Joseph was after all a pillar of the community with a sensible, intelligent wife. The winter wore into a late spring and people began to forget the scandal in preparation for the rush of the summer months.

There was a family up beyond Friar's Head which was starving and this weighed on the priest's mind much more than Dulcine LeBlanc. One by one they had lost all their cows to tuberculosis and the children had started to come to school pale-faced and ragged. Father Aucoin had discovered all this when the oldest had fainted during catechism and he had taken him up to the presbytery. The boy had eaten the hot cereal and milk as if he was starving and once the food was in his stomach began to brighten. The boy did not complain, but little by little the story had come out. The barrels of salted mackerel, the oatmeal, the potatoes and turnips, all the food put down for the winter was exhausted and now there was not even milk in the house. They had fallen from being well-off to scavenging for winter apples.

The priest listened to all this and the crease between his eyebrows deepened into a strong line. What to do? That was the question. You did not take food baskets to Frederic Cormier's house. He was too proud a man. Neighbours had tried it and been sent away from the door with a thanks and their food baskets still in hand.

Frédéric Cormier had been known as a great stockman. His cows had been big, beautiful brown and white Ayrshires. They had won prizes at the county fair. He had been as proud of them as he was of his own children. One night, the solution came to him and he walked immediately in the dead of night to the house of William à Joseph. He told him to go at first light and find the best cow in the county, not the second best, the best, the one that had won all the blue ribbons at the Fall Fairs, buy it and some good laying hens and take them up to Frédéric Cormier. He would pay for the cow and the hens, but Frederic should be told that they were paid for from a government program. This was done. William à Joseph delivered the cow, lied and Frédéric swallowed the lie because he loved the cow from the first moment that he saw her straight back, long body, and wide, capacious udder.

Winter passed into a bright spring. The Cormiers did well. The cow gave birth to twin calves and they became the start of a new herd. Dulcine's parents died. First the old Captain and then the wife, they went out like lights a few weeks apart. The funerals were quick, expeditious affairs. The Captain had had a big family, but the children had all long since left home and were so scattered it was difficult to find them. Dulcine was the chief mourner. She walked behind the coffin. The priest and the altar boys walked on ahead. She did not cry. Her face was simply still.

After the funeral, Father Aucoin invited her to the Presbytery for some tea, but she did not accept. She disappeared back into her little shack by the harbour.

This happened not long before the government decided to extend the harbour pier and William à Joseph was chosen as one of the foremen to supervise the work. They say this piece of luck was his and Dulcine's downfall.

The work was the hot, labouring kind where the men had to build cribs against the sea and then fill in behind with rocks. The young farmer began to stop at Dulcine's to chat and water his horses before going home. The stops began to get longer and this did not go unremarked by the postmistress who was supervising the construction work from her office on the hill. Soon, she felt obliged to go and tell the priest.

Father Aucoin ignored the postmistress. He had heard enough of her complaints about Dulcine, and so William à Joseph continued to stop at Dulcine's on his way home. Although how he had time for much more than a glass of water is hard to see, because his farm chores were waiting for him at home. Each night, he fell exhausted into bed only to be up again at six to start the next day's chores.

When the extension of the pier finished in September, William à Joseph continued to visit Dulcine. Whenever he went to the store or the fish plant or the Credit Union, he would also stop in to see Dulcine. The postmistress dutifully reported this new development to Father Aucoin and this time he did listen. William à Joseph was clearly not making much of an effort to avoid the occasion for sin. The crease between his eyebrows deepened. What to do? He relied on William à Joseph. He was one of the young men he depended upon to do the right things. The idea of losing the young man to sinful ways was unbearable to contemplate. It was William à Joseph who had found the cow for the Cormiers. It was William à Joseph who had devised the new crib works for the harbour. The man from the government had just stood around and watched. What to do? He chewed at the corner of his mouth until it bled. He did not want to do it, but what choice did he have? Sin was sin. He went to see the nuns.

The priest of St. Joseph de la Mer was not on the best of terms with the nuns in Cheticamp, whom he considered rather tiresomely holy. Nor were they that fond of Father Aucoin whom they also considered rather tiresomely holy. And there was the little matter of Father Aucoin's hillbilly students who regularly outdid their convent girls at the provincial exams. This was also irritating. Nonetheless, Father Aucoin was a priest and they were nuns and when he came to Cheticamp and asked them to fire Dulcine Leblanc, they did not hesitate. They let her go and found another girl to clean the floors.

Next, he called William à Joseph to the Presbytery. Father Simon did not mince his words. He told William à Joseph flat out that he had arranged for Dulcine to be fired and furthermore, there was no hope Dulcine would ever get a job at the hospital again and furthermore to the furthermore, there was not much point in him coming to confession in St. Joseph de la Mer because he would not grant William à Joseph absolution for his sin. There was no point, as it was clear William à Joseph was not making much of an effort to avoid the occasion for sin.

William à Joseph stopped visiting Dulcine. He would stay only at her door. He would not go inside the house. This the postmistress reported faithfully to Father Aucoin and anyone else who would listen. The witch would have to leave St. Joseph de la Mer, that was the opinion of the Post Mistress.

But Dulcine did not leave St. Joseph de la Mer. She stayed in her little cabin and the young farmer brought her wood when it began to be cold and Margaret sent her baskets of food. This created a great deal of gossip, but Dulcine herself was left strictly alone. She was a witch. No one but William à Joseph and Margaret Doucet would talk to Dulcine.

Winter set in. Christmas came and went. The time of the Chandeleur came round again. Father Simon banned it and this time he would not be moved. There was no Chandeleur. People blamed this on Dulcine and William à Joseph. Not a word passed from people's lips when she came to shop at the Co-op. Not a word when she came to church. She was ignored. Dulcine seemed to be shrinking back in her own eyes to that insubstantial figure on the shore.

The winter was long and hard, but Dulcine could be seen walking along the beach in all kinds of weather. She was always alone. In March, Dulcine could stand it no longer. She packed her things into one small suitcase, closed the door behind her and left St. Joseph de la Mer. William à Joseph drove her to the train station in Inverness and Dulcine Leblanc disappeared along with her brothers and sisters into the Boston States.

No one heard from her for years and years. Except in February at the time of the Chandeleur, she would send William à Joseph a story. They were written in a clear, even hand.

The Angelus

Venite, Exultemus Domino

The ewe disappeared the day that Philibert got drunk. Daniel searched for her from one end of the field to the other. She wasn't there. She wasn't hiding in the shade of the red currant bushes. She wasn't hiding in the wood lot. He'd been in every corner and crevice of the barn. He'd searched the fence line. There was no mark, no break where one pregnant ewe could have passed through.

"Then where was she?" asked Father Aucoin looking up from his desk, annoyed. "She had to be in the field. Look again."

"Perhaps she fell over the cliff," said Daniel. "It happens sometimes."

"No, I don't think so," said the priest thinking about this. "She's there somewhere."

Daniel went back to the field and began to walk in an aimless way back and forth across it. The cows and sheep began to trail after him. They made a curious picture, the boy walking in a desultory way, the little flock fanned out behind him.

Philibert arrived at the front door of the Presbytery playing his harmonica. He had the inclination to play long, tuneless dirges when he was drunk. He sat down with a clunk on the Presbytery stairs and waited. It didn't take long. His cousin emerged.

"I'd like to make a confession," announced Philibert without looking directly at the priest.

"Confessions are held on Tuesday and Thursday in the church, not on the Presbytery stairs," said Father Aucoin already exercising the virtue of patience.

"But that will be too late. By Tuesday, I may be a hardened sinner. I need to confess now when I am contrite and defeated. No, Tuesday will definitely be too late." Philibert shook his head with great exaggeration.

"Philibert, you've been defeated and contrite before."

"It's not entirely my fault. People take advantage of me. I'm easily led."

"That may be, Philibert, but I advise you to take yourself home."

"I don't want to go home. My wife will make me sleep in the barn."

"Wise woman."

"It's humiliating to sleep in your own barn. The neighbours will talk."

"If you don't want them to talk, don't drink."

"My wife treats me like a stray dog."

"So she should. If it were up to me, I'd put a collar on you and keep you chained up in the front yard."

"I don't understand. You're a priest. You're supposed to be solicitous to us poor sinners."

Philibert lay back on the couch and the entire sky began to revolve in a rather discouraging way. He sat up and then stood up and vomited vigorously, the entire contents of his stomach liberating themselves onto Father Aucoin's small flower bed.

"What a waste," said Philibert and sat down shakily on the porch stairs.

"Go down to the barnyard and wash yourself off in the horsetrough," said the priest. "That is, if the horse will let you."

Philibert wagged his finger at the priest. "See, you're disgusted with me. I can tell. I'm not. Not in the slightest. That's the trouble with you, cousin, you don't understand evil. It always surprises you. It never surprises me. On the contrary, what I find amazing is not that I am at present wretchedly drunk, but that I am so often stone, cold sober. This is what I find discouraging. It takes a great deal of effort to get this drunk. All I can think is that the devil must have a very weak grip on me."

"Shall I send for your wife to come and get you?"

"Oh no," said Philibert, his pale face becoming paler.

"What are you going to do?"

"Can I sleep in your barn? No one will know if I sleep here. Then I can go home quietly in the morning."

"I don't let smokers sleep in my barn. It's too dangerous."

"I don't have any cigarettes. Not one."

"Empty your pockets."

"I don't have any cigarettes left."

"Empty them."

Philibert emptied his pockets. One yellow, battered package of cigarette tobacco emerged, one package of papers; one box of all-weather wooden matches, fifteen cents and one pocket watch."

"I thought you said that you didn't have any cigarettes left?"

"I don't. Not one made."

The priest sighed. "You are not only a drunk Philibert, you are a liar and a corrupting moral influence."

"No doubt you're right, but can I sleep in your barn? I promise faithfully to be gone in the morning. I will be silent. No one but you will know I've been here."

"The boy will know, he does the chores."

"Daniel won't say anything. I know the lad."

"Why in heaven's name should I protect you? Go home, Philibert. Face your wife."

"Because it's not entirely my fault."

"Did someone force the rum down your throat?"

"It's not entirely my fault, that I'm not like you, cousin. It's not my fault that I didn't know at ten years old that I was going to be a priest."

"I didn't."

"Oh yes you did. I remember and don't you deny it, your father asked us at the dinner table what we were going to be when we grew up and you piped, 'I'm going to be a priest.' You said that at ten years old."

"I said it, Philibert, because he wanted some sort of an answer and it seemed like a reasonable thing to say."

"You didn't want to be a priest?"

"Not at ten."

"You just said it."

"I just said it."

"I always thought you were kind of born wanting to be a priest."

"No."

"Well, you are now."

"Yes."

"Where are you going?" called Philibert after the priest.

"I'm going to look for the boy. He's disappeared again."

Philibert nodded vaguely and just stood at the Presbytery porch holding with one hand onto the bannister. The priest stopped and came back. He picked up his cousin's tobacco and matches.

"Go sleep in the barn, Philibert."

Philibert nodded as if he had been expecting this all along and began to walk shakily towards the barnyard. He asked the horse if it would be all right to use his water trough. The horse did not seem to mind. Then he knelt down at the trough and washed his face for a long time. The water felt wonderfully clean and fresh, better than the whiskey.

Philibert climbed into the mow and bedded down comfortably in the loose hay. The world still revolved, but more slowly now. He dreamed that he was rich. He owned a great number of things, although he was not sure what, except that it was a good deal. There were blueberries and cream and fresh, strong tea. There was a Scottish girl who smiled at him. Yes, he was rich, so rich that he did not have a worry in the world.

Daniel had found the ewe. She had dropped her two little lambs in the depths of the red currant bushes, right beside a fox hole. The fox had butchered one already and the ewe was standing with a dazed expression on her face making futile little trots sometimes in the direction of the fox, sometimes in the direction of her remaining lamb.

The dead lamb was severed into pieces. By the time the boy found it, there was nothing but little pieces of bloody bone left. The fox had cracked the skull open and was carefully licking out the brains. It was a large dog fox with a flaming tail as long as its entire body. The ewe began to bleat feebly. It was as if there was something caught in her throat. She made a strangled sound. The newborn lamb, unaware of any danger, kept walking unsteadily towards the sheep's udder, but she ignored him, turning always to face the fox.

The fox nosed the remains of the dead lamb and then stood up, stretching comfortably from forelegs to hips. Then, he began to walk towards the second lamb which was standing alone and trembling, aware now something was wrong, but unable to understand what. The mother began to trot back and forth with bulging, vacant eyes. The fox stopped to watch her for a moment and then turned his attention back towards the lamb. He was like a cat with a particularly pleasing mouse. He wanted the lamb to run, but the little creature was too young. He still carried bloody marks from the birth.

Daniel came pushing through the bush and stumbled onto the scene. The fox looked up uncertain for a moment what to do. The ewe finally found her voice and began to bleat energetically. Daniel clapped his hands together making a short, sharp sound and then dove towards the lamb sweeping it up into his arms. The fox's lips curled back over his fangs and he was gone.

When the priest arrived, the boy was trying to get the lamb to suckle at the teat of the mother, but she would have nothing of it. She kept pawing stupidly at the remains of her first born and ignoring the second.

"You're going to get that lamb killed," said the priest. "She's going to kick him. What's the matter with her?"

"A fox killed the first one. She's frightened."

"I'll hold her, and you introduce the young one to dinner." The priest straddled the sheep pinning the animal between his knees. She stood still for a second and then began to kick and buck like a wild bronco. Now that the fox was gone and the danger was past, her little brain had decided to engage in a great and terrified fury. The priest was thrown to the ground and the ewe went bleating and bucking across the field to join the rest of the flock.

"This is not my day," said Father Aucoin, prying himself up to the elbows.

"What are we going to do with the lamb?" asked the boy, who was afraid that the little creature would die.

"We'll take him to the house and get Mrs. Cross to make a bottle for him." The priest stood up and dusted himself off.

"Can we give him a name?" asked Daniel, feeling the lamb's heart beating against his own.

"It's not normal to name something that you're going to eat," said the priest, thinking about this.

"We could keep him as a ram. We have no ram."

"We could," said the priest in an absent-minded way as he was trying to remember what he was annoyed about and could not. "What would you like to call him?" he asked, thinking of the problem of the name instead.

The boy considered this and did not reply immediately.

"How about a prophet?" asked the priest looking at the little lamb. "We could call him Amos. Amos was interested in justice and this little creature has suffered some rough justice."

The boy shook his head. "No," he replied, and then the name came to him. "I'd like to call him Philibert."

"Philibert the sheep?" said the priest, and Father Aucoin began to laugh. He laughed and laughed until tears sprang from his eyes.

Daniel had never seen the priest laugh like this before and he began to grow alarmed.

"Is there anything wrong?"

"Nothing at all. Nothing at all," replied the priest, still gasping. "I just love the name, Philibert, the sheep." And he started to laugh all over again.

The bell sounded from the church spire and the priest finally remembered what he had come to get the boy for. "The Angelus! We'll be late for the Angelus!" He hitched up his soutane and began to run across the hummocky pasture towards the church. The boy followed along, carrying the lamb.

Un Bargain à Jean à Basile

When Grandfather passed Jean à Basile's house, he would always crack the whip over the horse to make him step lively and he would sink a little into his coat as if Jean à Basile had the evil eye. Not that Jean à Basile's house was much to look at, you could hardly tell where the barn ended and the house started. The shingles of the house were grey like the barn, for Jean à Basile painted nothing. Paint cost money. The windows were covered with a thin checkerboard of this and that. It was the house of a pauper. When the doctor visited Jean à Basile's house, he felt sorry for him and charged him next to nothing which infuriated Grandfather, for Jean à Basile had money enough.

Sometimes, he would visit Grandfather and they would talk out by the woodpile. Now, there were many men who came to visit Grandfather because he had lived long and done a great deal. But Jean à Basile did not come to waste time talking. Jean à Basile had a horror of wasting time as deep as his fear of being cheated. He suspected the worst of his fellows and prepared himself accordingly.

Jean à Basile would buy nothing at the Co-op that was not marked down. He knew if it was not marked down, the store manager was cheating him. "Full price is for fools and rich men," said Jean à Basile and he bought the water-damaged oats, the jeans with a tear, the chocolate in the crushed package, until in St. Jean de la Mer, anything broken came to be known as a bargain à Jean à Basile.

One day, Jean à Basile's old horse fell down dead in his stall. It was the only horse that Jean à Basile owned. For twenty-five years, the same rack thin horse had done Jean à Basile's ploughing, harrowing, seeding, raking. The old horse pulled along from first light to day end on just enough hay to keep flesh over ribs. When he finally expired, Jean à Basile shipped him off to the fox farm in Margaree for a few dollars.

Anyway, the long and short of it was, Jean à Basile needed a new horse. That was why he had come to see Grandfather. He wanted a cheap horse, but one that was young, well-mannered and strong.

Grandfather leaned on his axe and thought about this for a time and then finally when Jean à Basile was hopping from foot to foot with anxiety, he said, "Sorry, I can't help you," and went back to splitting wood.

"What do you mean, you can't help me? Everyone knows you're an expert with horses."

Grandfather shrugged and said, "Why should I help you to find a horse to starve and overwork?"

"I don't starve my cattle."

"I wasn't talking about your cattle. I was talking about your horse. There's a difference."

"Of course there's a difference. You can sell a cow for money. You know what you get with a cow. A horse is nothing but trouble."

"Your old horse served you faithfully for twenty-five years, you call that trouble."

"And then he fell down dead in his stall. Never said a word, just keeled over and died. A cow wouldn't do that. Horses are trouble, that's why I want you to help me."

"Get your own horse and leave me in peace," said Grandfather, for he had never liked Jean à Basile.

"All I want is a good bargain. I don't want to be cheated."

"You don't want to be cheated!" yelled Grandfather sinking his axe in the splitting block with a thunk. "No, you want to do the cheating. You want to buy a horse that is young, strong, well-mannered and costs nothing."

"I said I wanted a bargain."

"That's not a bargain," steamed Grandfather. "That's robbery," and he stamped off to the house where Jean à Basile would not follow him.

But Jean à Basile did not give up easily and he came back the following evening as Grandfather was splitting wood for the kitchen stove. This time he did not bother with pleasantries.

"What kind of neighbour are you, William? I need your help. It costs you nothing but a bit of time and you won't give it to me."

Grandfather did not trust himself to reply.

"You tell me what to do and I will follow your advice. If you tell me to pay five hundred dollars for a horse, I'll pay it and no questions asked, no arguments made."

"Five hundred dollars is a lot of money. You don't have to pay that much," said Grandfather thinking about this and Jean à Basile sighed for he had finally sunk the hook in Grandfather's throat.

"Two hundred, five hundred, I just want to show that I trust you."

Grandfather struggled against it, but he could feel himself sliding towards helping Jean à Basile.

"What about shoes? Will you shoe the horse if I find you one?"

"I'll take her to the blacksmith every two months, rain or shine."

"Grandfather thought about the poor, skinny horse that Jean à Basile had driven for many years, often without shoes and wanted to say no, but he had a great passion for horses. To go looking for a horse was a great treat for Grandfather. It was in one way what his whole life had been about, for he had been a trader of horses in his youth, and a stallion keeper for many more. And the more that he had thought about clip clopping down farm lanes looking for the perfect horse to buy, the more he wanted to do it.

In the end, he told Jean à Basile that he would think about it, which was as good as saying he would do it.

Three days later, Grandfather found Jean à Basile a mare on a small holding up in the mountains behind Pleasant Bay. The mare was owned by an old woodsman who was closing down his mountain land and moving to Pleasant Bay. She was coal black, small, strong, and very quick. Grandfather liked her from the first instant that he saw her. She had wide-spaced eyes, a deep chest, a short strong back and high, muscular hindquarters. Grandfather said that he would buy her if Jean à Basile did not want her, which was the highest compliment that he could give.

Jean à Basile listened to Grandfather and he listened to the woodsman, but he did not entirely trust either, for buying a horse is a tricky thing. A horse that looks perfectly healthy in the day can have terrible heaves at night. A horse that looks sway-backed can be tough as iron while one that appears straight backed and strong can be weak-kneed and foundered. There is no end to the confusions. Horse trading is a job for gypsies and thieves. Jean à Basile felt sick for he knew as sure as eggs is eggs if he bought her, she would start coughing and fall down dead in her stall; and if he didn't he would regret it. He did not know what to do. He pulled at his hair in despair and stared grimly into her mouth. He felt her hocks and all the time the little mare stood patiently, as if she knew she was about to be sold to Jean à Basile, the greatest miser on the Inverness coast.

On the way home, the mare's lively step cheered Jean à Basile from the depression that he had sunk into from parting with his money and he began to tell himself what a fine deal that he had struck for the little mare. Grandfather kept his thoughts to himself.

It was on Sunday that Jean à Basile discovered his little mare was blind in one eye. She was stuck in a corner of the churchyard, and could not turn right because of a ditch and she would not turn towards her blind side. In a fury, Jean à Basile beat her to make her turn left, but she just lowered her head and stood quietly accepting the blows. She would not turn left. It was then Grandfather told Jean à Basile that the little mare was blind in one eye.

Jean à Basile began to curse. He cursed in front of Father Aucoin. He cursed in front of the whole village.

Grandfather smiled and said, "I thought you knew. I thought you wanted a bargain à Jean à Basile. That's why you got her so cheap."

When Jean à Basile heard this he turned red in the face, spittle gathered at the corners of his mouth, and his whole body trembled with rage. "You tricked me, William. I trusted you and you tricked me! You lied." Jean à Basile shook his finger in Grandfather's face two inches from Grandfather's nose.

"I did not lie. I said that I would buy her and I will."

Jean à Basile stopped cursing.

"You meant it?"

"Yes."

"The same price I paid?"

"The same price."

"Sold," said Jean à Basile and the whole village heard him. But the instant Jean à Basile said this, he began to regret losing his little black mare and he began to worry Grandfather was cheating him.

That evening, when Jean à Basile came to visit Grandfather, he was leading the little black mare.

"I have the money," said my grandfather.

But Jean à Basile shook his head. "I've changed my mind. I would like to keep her, but I want you to train her to turn left towards her blind side."

Grandfather leaned on his axe and thought about this and then he shook his head. "It can't be done. To turn left, she has to trust you."

"She will trust me."

"Horses don't trust people that beat and starve them."

"I don't beat her."

"What were you doing in the churchyard?" said Grandfather and went back to splitting his wood.

"I was angry," said Jean à Basile.

My Grandfather spat and went back to splitting wood.

"How much will you charge me to train her? I'll pay you good money," and Jean à Basile said this as if the words had been wrenched from his soul. But Grandfather did not bother to reply. He had had enough of Jean à Basile.

Now, Jean à Basile was many things, but one of the things he was not, was stupid. He had not gotten to be the richest man in the village by being a dolt. He went back to the little black mare and stroked her shining coat and then he came back to Grandfather and said, "I'll make you a deal, William. A good deal. I won't give you a penny, but if you can train her to turn left, without beating her, I'll give you her first foal."

Now, my grandfather was a great lover of horses and as soon as he heard Jean à Basile say this, he was already thinking of who the father of the foal might be. Jean à Basile had offered him the one thing that he could not refuse. They shook hands and the deal was sealed.

Grandfather left the little mare in the barn for several days. He took her out with our own horses but he did nothing except let her run along on a lead as if she was nothing more than a yearling and she began to grow playful. But she would not turn towards her blind side; no matter how he coaxed, she balked at this.

One morning, Grandfather hitched her to his two-wheeled cart and he began to make her turn to the right. He made her turn to the right until she became so tired her legs trembled and the traces were lined with lather and then Grandfather asked her to turn left towards her blind eye. The little mare was so relieved to turn left that before you could blink she had done it. After she had done this, she trembled even more and I thought that she might fall down altogether but she didn't and with that first turn it was as if a solid dam had burst in her mind. Each day, she turned a little more easily towards her blind side until she would turn left almost as quickly as right.

Jean à Basile was beside himself when he saw how easily his little black mare turned left. He jumped up and down and crowed to everyone who would listen, "I've got the best mare in all of Inverness County."

Grandfather said nothing, but he was already thinking of the foal that would soon be his.

The little black mare lived a long, useful life and became as familiar in St. Joseph de la Mer as Jean à Basile himself. Her quick step and proud carriage was recognised from Margaree Harbour to Cheticamp and people would say with an envious sigh, "Ah yes, that is the little mare that Jean à Basile got for next to nothing in Pleasant Bay. As for Grandfather, he never did get his foal because Jean à Basile never had her bred, and it came to be known that Grandfather had gotten a bargain à Jean à Basile.

The Bishop's Candlesticks

Christmas in St. Joseph de la Mer began at Advent. By then the boats had all been pulled up on the shore. The nets hung in the sheds. The turnips and potatoes had been pulled from the earth. Indian summer had played itself out. There were no more gentle reminders of summer days. Houses were sodded between the walls and ground. Those who could afford them put double windows on, and those who could not brought more wood in the house. Summer porches were closed in with planks. The last of the stove wood was stored in the shed, and the land settled into a grey stillness waiting for the first snow. The days brief, like a candle guttering out.

On the first of December, the women brought the Advent calendars out. They were hung by the stove, and peoples' minds began to turn towards Christmas and eating too much, and drinking too much, and getting cranky from too much company.

Late at night after the chores were done, the women baked fruit cakes, and meat pies, and cookies, and then hid them away in tin boxes, in remote, cold corners of the house where they would stay fresh, and little ones wouldn't find. The men began to buy candies at the Co-op, and secrete them away in tool shed, where they would ponder the Eatons Order catalogue trying to juggle what was wanted against what was needed. The fishermen began to sew wreaths of pine with fishing twine for the front door and garlands of ribbon pine for the stairs.

At the Presbytery, Father Aucoin and Mrs. Cross argued over where the Christmas tree should go. Father Aucoin thought the hall was about right. Mrs. Cross thought the library was about right. The choir began to practise 'Adeste Fideles,' and there was jockeying for solo parts. Anselme Chiasson would sing 'O Holy Night,' because he had the best voice in the village and it was the hardest tune. But everything else was hard felt. Sophie Deveau was ecstatic when Father Aucoin picked her to sing the Page in Good King Wencesles. Ulric Leblanc was devastated, as he was sure he would have made a better Page than Sophie Deveau who was freckled and small and a girl.

Philibert began to tune up his reading voice for: 'And it came to pass in those days, that there went out a decree from Caesar Augustus, that all the world should be taxed.' Although, he made it a point to tell anyone who wanted to listen that he didn't believe in God or Jesus Christ, but he felt obliged to read because his cousin asked him. (His cousin always asked him and Philibert always read.)

The church was strung with garlands of pine and spruce down the centre aisle, and red and green ribbons were tied there. Father Aucoin and the priest's boy, Daniel Boudreau set out a creche in front of the church. They brought the pieces out from the barn where they had been stored all year. It was freezing cold, and the boy's fingers chilled through his mittens, and his breath blew in a frosty cloud. The priest hummed as he carried the carvings out. He did not seem to mind the cold or hear the boy stamping his feet and banging his hands to keep warm.

The creche pieces had been commissioned by Father Aucoin from an old fisherman on Cheticamp Island. In the beginning, it had been another charity of the priest. Something to put a little money in the old man's pocket without him feeling the charity, but the old man had not died, and it began to be seen that his carvings were beautiful.

When he had finished the three wise men and Joseph and Mary, the fisherman, who was an old and fiercely independent man, began to carve likenesses of people that he knew. He began with the pretty figure of Margarite Poirier who had lived for many years in a small house overlooking the harbour. The next year, the fleshy face of Albert à Didier, the hotel keeper of St. Joseph de la Mer was added. The sardonic visage of Philibert, the matchmaker, came next, and at the back of the crowd the thin curve of the village miser, Jean à Basile, holding tight to his little, black mare was seen.

The priest who had not asked for these village reprobates to be in the creche scene argued against them. He did not want to pay for them. There were more worthy persons in the village, and then the fisherman looked up from his work bench and said simply, "is it only worthy people who can come to the child's birthday?"

When he heard this, the priest felt ashamed of himself. From that day forward they did not argue, and Father Aucoin began to understand the old fisherman was creating a history of the village in his creche scene. For over the years, a throng of silent figures began to gather around the creche: fishermen and farmers, sisters and housewives crowding around the little manger in a circle that spilled beyond the corner of the church.

This year's addition was an altar boy singing from his hymnal dressed in his surplice. He looked like an angel, an angel in the image of Daniel Boudreau. It was the priest's curious Christmas gift to the boy, although the boy did not understand this. He did not understand it was the priest who had chosen him, not the old fishermn. He said nothing, but he wondered. There was a long line of boys who had been great successes at the Presbytery. His older brother, Robert had won a university scholarship in Halifax. Why had the old man not chosen him? The boy was proud, and at the same time uneasy when he looked at his wooden likeness singing among the other wooden people.

At the centre of the creche, scarcely visible through the crowd were the three wise men who were dark and bearded wearing brightly painted clothes of blue and gold and red. Mary and Joseph were in sober browns and white and the baby was tucked away in a trough of straw and so bundled up, one could scarcely see whether it was white, black or shellacked. (Father Aucoin took the biblical direction of swaddling seriously.) The entire scene was lit by two hurricane lamps which hung from the corners of the makeshift shed and sent out two comforting yellow beams up and down the main street of the village.

Father Aucoin and the boy put the creche up the Sunday before Christmas, and from that moment on the baking and mending and building of wooden toys in St. Joseph de la Mer began to race at fever pitch towards the finish line of Christmas Eve.

Children woke early to mark the days off on December gleefully, and adults were too busy to notice the sun had faded to a spark in the sky, and the southeast gales howled down the coastline and rattled the window panes.

Throughout Advent, there would be a terrible coming and going in the Presbytery as choristers, and actors in the pageant, and visitors dropped by on their way to or from the church. Mrs. Cross would have a permanent kettle boiling on the stove and pans and pans of gingerbread in the oven. For the boy, the smell of Christmas was always the sweet scent of gingerbread, and the crackle of parcels being set down in the Hall. There would be a holler from the porch, the front door would swing open, and the sound of a thud would reverberate through the house as something hit the floor. The door would then swing shut, and a mysterious brown package would be found sitting in the hall.

Invariably, Father Aucoin would say, 'ah, Father Christmas has arrived early this year' and he would pick up the parcel, and set it down on the dining room table without opening it, which was a great frustration to the boy.

Father Aucoin's temper which was short at the best of times, at Christmas would begin to seriously fray. The choir sounded wretched. The Bishop's candlesticks had not arrived as promised. The children could not seem to remember their lines for the pageant. The Christmas tree had gone up in the study as Mrs. Cross had wanted, instead of the Hall where Father Aucoin had wished.

The one day a brown package from Boston arrived and Father Aucoin shook it this way and that and decided to open it up there and then. The boy felt a great bubble of excitement in his chest. Mrs. Cross gave him the scissors, and there was much snipping of string and tearing of paper. The boy kept lifting the box trying to figure out what could be inside, but he could see and feel nothing even after he had opened it. Inside the box, there was nothing but crumpled newspaper. Lots of newspaper crumpled up, and he kept taking the newspaper out until he found neatly packed in the middle, small boxes of red and white candy canes.

"There must be a hundred," said the boy astonished at the size of his treasure chest.

Father Aucoin picked the boxes up and said cryptically "come with me." He put on his coat and boots and they crossed the yard to the church. "I thought we'd hang them from the boughs," he said to the boy. "Do you think God would mind?"

"Who will eat them?" asked Daniel, being practical.

"I thought the children would. They could take them home after Mass."

"I don't know," said the boy uncertain because he had nourished the brief and greedy hope that they were all for him.

"Well, I think we had better try one first, don't you? To make sure that they taste as they should," said the priest and he took one of the candy canes out of the box, and stuck it in his mouth. The boy did the same, and sat down in the pew opposite the priest. Neither said anything more for a few moments. The priest was tired and so was the boy. The candy canes were peppermint and tasted just fine to both of them.

"It looks nice," said the priest finally breaking the silence with a small gesture of his candy can towards the altar which had crisp white linen on it and green boughs around the base. There was another long, comfortable silence.

"I think I will put the Bishop's candlesticks in the centre of the altar," said the priest thinking about his candle sticks, for they were on his mind. The Bishop had never sent a gift or present of any kind to St. Joseph de la Mer, but this year there had been a little hand-written note scrawled in the November, monthly circular. *"Will be sending Bishop's candlesticks for Christmas, — G."*

Father Aucoin had been thrilled by this note for there were some beautiful candlesticks in the Basilica, and they had very little in St. Joseph de la Mer. They would make a wonderful ornament to the liturgy of the Mass.

Whenever he thought of the new candlesticks he felt like humming. They would need large candles and he was already turning over in his mind where they might find some that would be adequate.

The boy looked up at the altar, and the windows above, and with the callowness of youth did not feel that the two of them were sitting alone in a very small boat balanced on the edge of vast seas. He felt only that it was late, and he would like to get to bed to sleep away the dreaming night, but he dared not move, because he knew the priest did not like to be disturbed in the church.

The priest finished his second candy cane and sighed. Christmas was almost here once more. The boy was growing up. He would have to see about getting him placed somewhere. Perhaps at St. Anne's or Boston, he must write to both of them, and he must write to his brother and thank him for the candy.

He got down on his knees and began his evening prayers. He sometimes felt guilty praying. Prayers were so easy, so comforting. It was harder to write letters.

He found the boy outside arranging the hay in the creche. They blew out the hurricane lanterns, and walked quietly back to the Presbytery together. The stars spilling across the sky between the mountains and the sea.

On Christmas Eve, Daniel's father Marcel Boudreau brought his youngest son's present to the Presbytery and tucked it under the tree. The Bishop's present arrived, and Mrs. Cross also tucked it under the tree. After midnight mass, faces flushed from rum and egg nog, meat pie and butter cookies, they gathered in the study to open the presents. With a yell of delight, Daniel pounced upon the stilts that his father had made for him, and immediately began stumping around the Presbytery teetering backwards and forwards with his father laughing, delighted and no one seeming to mind.

The priest opened his present from the Bishop. It was a small book called *The Bishop's Candlesticks*. It was a play. On the inside cover, a brief note was scrawled from the Bishop saying he had enjoyed it, and perhaps Father Aucoin might also. As usual, he signed it, simply 'G.'

The priest held the book in his hand as if it was a small and very heavy weight. "Very thoughtful of the Bishop," he said. "Very thoughtful." He watched the boy swaying around on his new stilts and was grateful for the lad's high spirits.

Just before the sun came up, Marcel Boudreau went home loaded down with Christmas food from Mrs. Cross, and they all went to bed except for the priest who went out to serve early morning mass for those who had missed the Midnight service.

The boy came with him although his head was nodding with happy fatigue. On his way into the church, the priest stuck *The Bishop's Candlesticks* under the arm of one of the wooden wise men, then he changed his mind and stuck it under the arm of Philibert, the Matchmaker.

The sun was coming up. Like a storm at sea, another Christmas season had been weathered. The priest felt rather fine, as if he had said enough prayers, as if God were pleased.

Miracle Potatoes

Father Aucoin was not happy with Daniel eating Sunday dinner *chez la famille* Cormier. Théophile Cormier was not from the improving side of the parish. He was one of those eternal talkers who ran everyone's business better than his own, including Father Aucoin's. Fortunately, while Théophile was busy saving the world from ineptitude, his wife was busy feeding his children.

When Théo rolled his cigarettes and considered the state of the universe his wife tended an enormous garden. When Théo walked down to the harbour to cadge a few cod from the fishermen, his wife was churning butter or knitting or preserving. Madame Cormier kept her girls fed and clothed through dint of hard work and re-used wool. The only thing that Théophile did with any efficiency was make children. He had seven girls, all of them beautiful, which was the reason Father Aucoin suspected Daniel wanted to have dinner there.

Before Daniel left, the priest went over his list of chores: the barn, the church, homework, piano practice. But they had all been done, and it was Sunday. There was no reason the boy could not go. Mrs. Cross gave him a large hamper of food to take to Mrs. Cormier's, and the boy set out down the lane towards the Cormiers.

Madame Cormier opened the door when Daniel arrived. Théophile was already preaching to a large assembly at the Sunday table. She picked up the basket and began to lay out the food Mrs. Cross had packed, strawberry preserves, scones, buns, cream, butter, and jars of soup ready to serve. Madame Cormier shook her head admiringly.

"And this, she told me to make sure you got this," and the boy reached into the basket and took out a large bar of chocolate. "It's chocolate," said Daniel, unsure of what to make of Mrs. Cormier's astonished expression. "It comes from the Boston States. Father Aucoin's sister sent it."

"It's pretty," said Mrs. Cormier, turning the sleek tablet over in her hands. The girls got up from the table and gathered around their mother each anxious to touch and see the Boston chocolate. The wrapping was dark brown and it had CADBURY'S MILK CHOCOLATE written in yellow-gold.

"Bah, sit down at the table," called Théophile, annoyed at his family. "A bar of chocolate is not a miracle. Come, the food is getting cold."

The girls went back to the table, and Mrs. Cormier set the chocolate down on its side in the middle of the table so that everyone could see it.

"Daniel, will you say grace?" asked Mrs. Cormier. The boy crossed himself and said grace, the words coming out with practised ease. When he looked up, Elodie was staring at him and he felt his face flush to the roots of his hair.

"So Daniel, are you going to be a priest like Father Aucoin?" asked Théophile, watching the boy blush.

"No," said the boy.

"Why not? You'll get chocolate from the Boston States. A nice, big Presbytery to live in, and someone to cook your meals and all you have to do is look prayerful. You do a pretty good job already."

"Don't tease the boy, Théo. It's not fair."

"I'm not teasing him, Jeanine. I'm delighted to hear Daniel doesn't intend to become a priest, there are entirely too many priests in the world already."

"What should he become?" asked Elodie, curious.

"A millionaire."

"But he has to do something to become a millionaire."

"Absolutely and that's for Daniel to decide. All I'm saying is that if Daniel wishes to marry one of my daughters, he will have to be a millionaire first. One poor man in the family is enough."

"Théo, I asked you not to tease the boy."

"I'm not teasing, I'm stating a fact. Each one of my daughters is worth a million dollars. They're not going to marry for anything less, right Daniel?"

The boy's face went a deeper scarlet.

"How do you like working at the Presbytery, Daniel? I have the feeling that you don't like it much."

"Théophile!" cried Mrs. Cormier, exasperated with her husband.

This time it was Elodie's turn to blush, for she had told her father this.

"Pardon, I didn't mean to pry," said Théophile and he calmly resumed eating his soup. The girls looked at Daniel surreptitiously, who countered by refusing to look up from his soup plate. It was confusing to be in the same room with so many pretty girls.

"The problem with this parish is we have no miracles. If we had miracles, we would all be millionaires. I'm serious. Jeanine, if Ste. Anne de Beaupré can have miracles, why can't St. Joseph de la Mer? Ste. Anne is just a little village in the middle of nowhere, and they have miracles by the ton. They have a great basilica, a hostel for pilgrims, if you don't believe me ask Marguerite à Medoc. She will tell you. She went there for a cure. And what do we have? A tiny little church and no one ever comes here who is not related. If I was the priest, the first thing I would do is have a few miracles, and then write to the Bishop to get them publicised in the Diocesan News. Then — Bingo, we'd all be on easy street."

"What kind of miracles?" asked the boy cautiously.

"Oh, the regular kind, curing the lame, seeing the virgin, that sort of thing."

"Théophile Michel Cormier you are being blasphemous, blasphemous in front of the children."

"How am I being blasphemous? I'm saying we need a few miracles around this little parish. Why is that blasphemous? We have a priest who is supposed to be saintly, and what miracle has he ever done? Name me one! Brother André in Montreal does miracles by the thousands. People come from all over Canada to get themselves cured by Brother André. There's miracles galore at Ste. Anne de Beaupré and what do we get? Sermons and piano lessons. I tell you in all honesty, Jeanine, if I was the priest, and I prayed as much as Father Aucoin, we would have miracles in St. Joseph de la Mer as sure as we are all sitting here."

"I don't know if Father Aucoin believes in miracles," said the boy thinking about this.

"See, what did I tell you? How can we have miracles in St. Joseph de la Mer if our priest doesn't believe in them? He won't even pray to move the ice off the fishing grounds which is a sin if you ask me," said Théophile pouring gravy expertly onto his potatoes as he said this.

"He believes in some miracles," said Elodie, "doesn't he, Daniel?"

"Yes, he believes it is a miracle that your mother married your father."

Elodie rewarded Daniel with a grin.

Théophile hooted. "That wasn't a miracle, Elodie, that was just bad judgment on your mother's part. She could have married Albert à Didier and she'd be rich today."

Jeanine Cormier made a wry expression in her husband's direction, but said nothing.

"What is a miracle, then?" asked Elodie.

"A miracle is something that makes money," said her father firmly.

"That's not what Father Aucoin says," said the boy, stubbornly resisting the dominating tone of the older man.

"Oh yes, then what does he say?"

The boy shrugged. "He says miracles are little things like Elodie playing the piano."

"Then we have several miracles in this house because Bernadette and Mathilda can play the piano also, and we don't even own one. No, that's childish nonsense, miracles are described in the Bible and it doesn't say a word about playing the piano. A miracle is curing the lame, making the blind see, raising the dead, those kinds of things. If I woke up in the morning and found the stones in my front pasture had changed to potatoes that would be a miracle, a real miracle. And you know what, Daniel? Your priest is afraid of real miracles, because he's afraid he's not good enough for them. That's why he spends all his time with little miracles," he gestured towards Elodie, "because he's afraid of the big ones. If I was a priest, I'd let the little miracles take care of themselves and concentrate on the big ones, the ones that make money." By this time, Théophile was wagging his finger at the boy, lecturing him from his considerable height, and the boy kept his thoughts to himself.

"Ahh, Papa, how you talk," said Elodie sighing.

"Can we have the chocolate now?" asked Mathilda, who was the youngest.

"With the strawberries, you have chocolate with strawberries, not potatoes, Mathilda," said Madame Cormier smiling.

It was during the lecture from Théophile Cormier that the boy first thought of planting potatoes in the Cormiers' front field, and the more he thought about it, the more he liked the idea. He and Ulric Chiasson could make a miracle without any trouble at all.

On his way back to the Presbytery, he stopped at Ulric's and explained his idea for a potato miracle. Ulric's father had a big farm and more potatoes than he knew what to do with. He wouldn't miss a sack or two; that same night, Daniel harnessed the old mare to the cart, and took her over the grass so her shoes would not make a sound. Only when he was at some distance from the Presbytery did he go down the road to the Cormiers'.

He and Ulric worked like slaves picking stones and planting new potatoes. Then just before the sun came up, they went home. Daniel didn't even bother to go into the Presbytery. He just started milking the cow and then came in with the pails of milk. Mrs. Cross took one look at his dirty face and sent him upstairs for a bath.

He fell asleep in early morning mass and Father Aucoin gave him hell. He said he wasn't well. This was the best way of dealing with Father Aucoin. He understood sickness and Daniel went willingly to bed where he slept until the afternoon.

On Saturday, two of the Cormier girls were flying a brown paper kite in the front field and when one ran to pick it up, discovered new potatoes there where it had fallen and then they began to find more and more. There were whole rows of them and the stones seemed to have disappeared.

The news travelled up to the Cormiers' and around the Parish like a thunder clap. By the end of the day, everyone from Friar's Head to Chéticamp knew that stones had been turned to new potatoes in Théophile's front field.

"It was a miracle! A real miracle!" cried Théophile Cormier. "Imagine, my prayers have been answered." And like a man possessed, he harvested his potatoes, working away with a shovel and fork. No one had ever really seen Théophile work before and people watched his performance in amazement. He would let no one else near his potatoes, not even his wife and daughters.

No one really believed that they were miracle potatoes, but then no one really believed that they weren't either. If someone had planted them in the dead of night, it would not have been easy, because Théophile's front field was right beside the road in plain view of the presbytery.

Théophile came cap in hand to the presbytery to ask Father Aucoin to write to the Bishop in Antigonish to inform him of the great news. Stones had been changed to potatoes in St. Joseph de la Mer! It needed to be published in the Diocesan News. A subscription should be taken up to build a Cathedral, just like in St. Anne de Beaupré. It should be a huge cathedral with stained glass and an enormous bell tower. The windows should look out onto the field and onto the sea. Théophile had it all planned out. He was ready.

God had finally answered his prayers. A miracle had happened in St. Joseph de la Mer.

But Father Aucoin would not write to the Bishop.

Théophile said Father Aucoin was jealous. God paid no attention to the priest, but he had answered his prayers. He had given him, Théophile Cormier, a miracle and nothing to the priest.

Father Aucoin did not argue with Théophile. There were no sermons from the pulpit on the nature of miracles. He said nothing for or against Théophile's miracle, but he would not write to the Bishop.

Théophile sent Philibert, the Matchmaker, to speak with Father Aucoin. Philibert was the priest's first cousin and had influence with him. Nothing came of it.

Albert à Didier came cap in hand. If the miracle could be confirmed he predicted a great future for his hotel. He would be able to employ more people. He would need cooks and waitresses and chambermaids and on and on it went. Father Aucoin listened patiently to Albert à Didier who had influence with the Bishop in Antigonish and said, "Next year, let's wait until we see what happens next year." He said this so gently that Albert à Didier could not reproach him.

Théophile grew frantic. The Virgin didn't appear every year. "Why should stones be changed into potatoes every year?"

The Doucet boys opened a potato stand of their own just down the road from Théophile and a great argument immediately erupted between Théophile and the Doucets. Théophile said the Doucets were not selling genuine miracle potatoes. The Doucets said their potatoes were merely souvenir potatoes. Théophile said they were not souvenirs. Only souvenirs of miracle potatoes could be sold from his stand.

The more frantic, the more greedy people became, the calmer the priest became. Then Théophile did something really extraordinary. He bought his girls a piano from the proceeds of his miracle potatoes. This news was almost as amazing as the appearance of the potatoes. Father Aucoin was invited to view this new piano at the Cormiers', and he accepted, dressed in his best soutane, with his shoes polished and his hair carefully combed. Mrs. Cross dressed the boy so that he too, would reflect well on the Presbytery, and the two of them walked off towards the Cormiers' as if prepared for a state occasion.

The gleaming new piano stood like a machine from Mars in the battered dining room of the Cormiers' little house. Father Aucoin was invited to play and he played for a long time, almost an hour. Whatever else one said about Father Aucoin, he could play the piano. He could make it sound like angels' wings.

Madame Cormier served tea and little cakes, and then Elodie Cormier played, not for long, but afterwards people said that she had played as well as Father Aucoin. Daniel Boudreau, the priest's boy was asked to play also, but he refused and the piano, being thus blessed, passed onto others.

Towards the end of the evening, Father Aucoin announced that he would write a letter to the Bishop telling him about the potato field miracle. He said he would say only what he knew to be true, that Bernadette and Mathilda had found potatoes in their father's front field, and that no one would admit to planting them. He would show the letter to Albert à Didier before he sent it, so there would be no misunderstanding later about what he had said. He wanted to say only the truth, not consecrate anything, that was not for him to do.

Théophile was overjoyed. He could not say enough fine things about Simon Aucoin, R.P. The priest blushed a little and said if Théophile Cormier could find it in his heart to buy his daughters a piano, he could find it in his heart to write a letter to the Bishop.

Théophile drank gallons of strong tea and made great plans. First, he must go to Ste. Anne de Beaupré and see what they had built there. He would go as a simple pilgrim and have a real experience, and then he would talk to the Bishop of Québec. "Ahh, there was so much to do."

Elodie tried to persuade her friend Daniel to play, but the boy could not be persuaded even by Elodie. He ate very little. He and his friend, Ulric Chiasson were the only unhappy notes at the party. The two of them sat in a kind of droopy silence together, talking little, seeming pale and drawn. The priest said the boy had lately been sickly.

Around midnight, the party began to break up and people began to go their own way home. As usual the priest and the boy were the first to go because they had early morning mass to serve. On the way home, the priest drove the buggy and the boy rehearsed how he would say it. In the end, he just said as the priest turned off the main road towards the Presbytery, "Ulric and I planted the potatoes."

Father Aucoin pulled the mare up short and the buggy shuddered to a halt.

"You what?"

"Ulric Chiasson and I planted the potatoes. We got the potatoes out of his father's barn and planted them at night."

"Why?"

"Théophile was talking about how a miracle had to make money. Ulric and I thought we would make a miracle for him. It was supposed to be a joke."

The priest sighed and loosened the reins on the mare who was anxious to go the last little distance to the barn.

"Whose idea was it?"

"Mine."

The priest said nothing more. Normally, it was the boy's chore to unhitch the mare, but this time the priest helped him. All the time, the boy became increasingly nervous until his head pounded and his stomach felt sick with a fever.

"Has Ulric told anyone?" the priest asked finally.

"No, he's afraid to."

"Not even his parents."

"No one, he was waiting for me to tell you."

"Can he keep a secret?"

"Yes."

"Then you should, for the moment, tell no one."

"Why?"

"Because," said the priest, pausing, "Théophile will lose his dream and some income. Both are important to him."

"But what about the Basilica and the hostel for the pilgrims," said the boy, confused.

"They won't get built, that is all, that is all," said the priest without a trace of sadness in his voice. "And in the meantime, the Cormier girls will have a piano which is a miracle of sorts. I will write to a friend of mine in Boston and see if we can find a scholarship for Elodie."

The priest looked at his watch. "Time for bed, young man."

The boy went to bed without another word of reprimand. He slept fitfully. He had expected that the priest would fall on him like the wrath of God; instead, he had seemed almost amused. Daniel did not understand. He played his scales a fraction too fast and the priest bellowed at him like a gored bull. He turned the entire parish upside down with miracle potatoes and he said, "time for bed, young man."

In his study, the priest wrote a long letter to his friend in Boston explaining how he had two excellent students who deserved and needed a musical scholarship to continue their studies. Then he wrote a short letter to the Bishop explaining about the Miracle Potatoes and apologising profusely. He blamed himself. He did not show the letter to Albert à Didier.

The Bishop replied immediately. He was not pleased. He asked his priest again to stay away from the Fisherman's Co-op and to concentrate on the spiritual life of the community. The spiritual life of the community did not include playing God with potatoes. He requested Father Aucoin to resign from the Board of the Credit Union and to include three novenas in his prayers as penance.

The young priest was grateful to have gotten off so lightly, resigned from the Board and said his novenas each evening with thankfulness.

Théophile visited Ste. Anne de Beaupré. He took the train from Inverness all the way to Québec City and then a bus to Ste. Anne. He came back with all kinds of great plans for St. Joseph. But the Bishop never came to the village and there never was a notice in the Diocesan News of the potato field miracle. Théophile blamed the priest. He said they could have all been rich if they had a real priest in St. Joseph. The priest said nothing.

Towards the end of Théophile's life when people had forgotten all about their own dreams of cathedrals and pilgrims and hotels, Théophile was thought of as a bit of a crank, and his grandchildren would be warned not to mention the subject of miracles.

Except after the potato field miracle, people in St. Joseph de la Mer separated miracles into two types, *"un miracle à Théo,"* which came to mean something extraordinary like winning the Loto and *"un miracle Aucoin,"* which came to mean something ordinary like the birth of a baby; and this distinction endured long after Théo Cormier and Father Aucoin had passed on.

Philibert and God

What good does a close association with God do you? I never saw a sense to it myself. Have you ever seen a happy priest? They all look like they've just swallowed a lemon, every one of them. Go to the presbytery if you don't believe me and look at the photographs. They all look the same. Old Father Poirier looks like his mother died on Monday and his sister on Tuesday. Father LeVert looks like a basset hound that missed his breakfast. His Eminence, Monsignor Richard, looks like the Pope asked him to teach catechism to some serious-minded mules. There isn't one of them that looks like he's getting a great deal of fun out of being holy.

So what's the point? You might as well go to the devil, at least you'll go laughing.

Ah, I did not say that Father Aucoin is not an exceptional man. *Sans doute*, he's exceptional. I've always thought so. He's the only priest we've ever had who doesn't look like he's sucking on a lemon. He looks hopeful. He's almost smiling. You would almost swear the corners of his mouth turn up. But mostly he looks wary as if he is a young boy who has just written his exams. He must be thirty-six or thirty-seven in the photograph and he looks twelve. Would you want to be twelve years old for the rest of your life?

Now, where was I? I was talking about Chloe à Euclide. Isn't that the woman you're interested in? She's the widow who lives at Point Cross overlooking the harbour. Three children, dark hair, blue eyes, a little thin.

No, that wasn't it. I was talking about God. Why do people want to be close to God? The answer is simple enough. It's because God is always right and people love to be right. Did you ever notice that? The closer that a person gets to God, the more often he or she is right.

Take Isabet à Robert, for example. She's just like Moses. Never wrong. She bakes perfect cookies. She's generous to a fault. Her house is perfectly clean. Her husband is perfectly behaved. He doesn't drink. Stays quiet when he's supposed to be quiet. Talks when he's supposed to talk. He's perfect but then he has to be, he lives with Isabet.

Isabet goes to early morning mass six days a week. Six days a week and high mass on Sunday! I wouldn't be surprised if God was giving her directions just like he did for Moses. Do this. Don't do that. Even Father Aucoin is careful how he addresses Isabet à Robert.

That's what being close to God is all about. You get to be right and that, my friend, is why priests look so sour. They're always so busy being right that it squeezes their soul into a lemon. The better the priest, the sourer he is.

As for me, God makes me nervous. I go to church only because my wife makes me. She would kick me out of the house if I didn't go to Mass on Sunday. So I go. I go and I pray. I pray that God will leave me alone.

I'm playing the fool? I am and I am not. Of course, it's not quite that simple. No doubt, I'm exaggerating. There are some advantages to riding in the same car as God. People tend to remember Moses. His name is carved on our souls, just like Father Aucoin's is carved on yours. No wonder, these guys make the rules and we have to follow them. How many wives did Moses have? How many battles did he fight against the Philistines, but what do we remember about Moses? We remember that he was close to God. We remember God gave Moses the Ten Commandments.

Remember the time that Father Aucoin walked all the way to Cheticamp to administer the last sacrament for Johnny Burns? Of course, you do. It was a howling day in January. Blowing so hard that you couldn't keep a car on the road and what happened? Father Aucoin caught pneumonia and Johnny Burns, the ingrate, refused to die. This is seen as an amazing thing. It doesn't seem so extraordinary to me.

You see these old legs on Philibert the Matchmaker? They've walked more miles in a month than Father Aucoin has in a year. I've walked from Pleasant Bay to Cap Rouge, to Cheticamp, to St. Joseph, to Margaree, and not the harbour, the Forks, and back again in a week. I've been in houses that Father Aucoin has never heard of and places he's preached about but never seen; bootlegger camps in the mountains, seal harvest sheds at Fishing Cove and everywhere I go, I am made welcome. Everywhere I go, there's always a place at the table for Philibert the Matchmaker.

But who will whisper stories about Philibert the Matchmaker when these old legs no longer carry me from house to house along the coast? No one, that's who, but mark my words when Father Aucoin finally moves into the driver's seat, mothers will whisper stories to their children about him. They will tell stories in hushed tones about the priest who died so poor the parish had to take up a collection to make sure he did not go to his grave in a pauper's shroud. For, no doubt, he will die a pauper because he gives every cent that he has for one fool project or another. You watch, he will become a local Moses.

So much for God. With any luck, I'll remain unnoticed and win the Irish Sweepstakes.

Ah yes, Chloe à Euclide. Take my advice as if your life depended on it. Forget what Father Aucoin said about her. Wipe it from your mind. He would not recognise a good woman if he fell over her at mid-day. He is a bachelor, a real bachelor. His head is full of angels. Fortunately for us, women are not angels.

Take Chloe à Euclide flowers. Find her some oranges. Beg her to marry you. Spare nothing for she is a woman who can make you happy.

Why do I know this? I know it because I've arrived at that unhappy age when a man knows nothing or everything about the human heart and I know everything, but too late, my friend, too late.

Une Chanson à Mederic

a folktale, *d'après Dulcine Leblanc*

"The devil plays the fiddle, everyone knows that. That's why we have so many fiddle players in Cape Breton. I can't imagine that God plays the fiddle. God plays the organ. Anyway, this story is about a fiddle player.

The fiddle player in this story was named Mederic. He was not a very good fiddler. He could play simple tunes, but he did not have the knack. He was always practising. He practised so much and played so little that there was a joke in the village which women used on their husbands when they were loafing. It was called playing '*une chanson à Mederic.*'

One Sunday afternoon, Mederic was walking home from the church hall with his fiddle case under his arm and he came upon an old farmer who was standing by his farm gate. The farmer, seeing the fiddle case under Mederic's arm invited the fiddler to play at a kitchen dance he was having.

Mederic shook his head and said no, as he always did when someone asked him to play at a dance. He would have loved to play, but his sense of rhythm was not sure enough to keep time for dancers. He told the farmer this, but the farmer smiled and insisted that he come anyway.

'But it's Sunday,' said Mederic suddenly remembering. 'Who has a dance on Sunday?'

'Ach, it's just myself and a few friends doing a little step dancing. It's not really a party at all.'

Mederic shook his head again. He was tempted, but he had promised his wife that he would only practise for an hour or so before coming home.

'Come in for a few minutes,' said the old farmer. 'It will be nice to have a change of fiddlers, if only for a few moments.'

'Would three tunes be enough?' asked Mederic, thinking about it.

'That would be plenty,' replied the old farmer with an even wider smile.

'All right,' said Mederic and he followed the old farmer down the lane towards a little white house. They went around to the back of the house and through a small door that you had to bend down to get past. Inside, there was a fiddler playing and a step dancer dancing. The room was quite dark. It looked very lonely and dreary, not like a dance at all. The fiddler began to get fearful. He wanted to go home to his wife and children but the old farmer wouldn't let him.

'You have to play now,' the farmer said. 'We want to hear you.'

So the fiddler stood up and played with the other man while the step-dancer danced on. It was the most awful screeching that you could imagine, but they wouldn't let him stop, he had to play on and on until finally he said, 'No, that's enough. I won't play anymore. I'm going home,' and he picked up his fiddle case and left.

He ran home as fast as he could go, but when he got there, it was too late. His house had rotted right down to the sills. There was nothing left but rocks in the ground to mark where the basement of his house had been. His wife and boys were gone from the neighbourhood. His fields had gone to wild seed. His barn roof sagged in the middle where the cross beam had broken. While Mederic had been playing his tunes in the old farmer's house, eighty years had passed by.

Mederic walked around the remains of his house in terrible despair. He could have sworn only twenty minutes had gone by in the farmer's house, for he had only played three or four tunes.

Not knowing what else to do, he walked back to the house where he had played and stood at the farm gate for a long time afraid to walk down the lane and afraid to leave. After a while a woman who was driving by, seeing Mederic in his old-fashioned clothes, stopped to ask him if anything was wrong, so he asked the woman about the small house at the end of the lane.

'It's just a wreck,' replied the woman. 'No one has lived there for years. You hear noises from it at night. I'm surprised that it hasn't burned down.' And she drove off.

Mederic looked at the house and knew with a sudden clunk of his heart that he had met the devil. In great fear, he began to walk slowly down the lane towards the house. He was trembling from head to foot when he got to the house, but he pushed open the small door at the back of the house and sure enough the devil was playing the fiddle. His face was fiery red and he cackled like a rooster as he played. From his head grew a horse's mane and a scaled tail swung from his backside.

A poor step dancer trapped by the devil's music was dancing in the middle of the room. The dancer's eyes were shut, sweat ran down from his forehead and his feet moved in a simple two-step over and over again.

'Play, play,' cackled the devil.

Mederic, with his heart thundering and his hands shaking, picked up his fiddle to play.

Now, it was well-known in the neighbourhood that while Mederic didn't play well, what he played he could fiddle backwards as well as forwards. And this is just what Mederic did. He stood in the middle of the Devil's kitchen and he played his tunes backwards. This made the most horrible sound imaginable, for the harder Mederic played his tunes backwards, the harder the devil played his tunes forward. The sound was so awful that time stopped and then started slowly to reverse itself.

The devil understood the game that the fiddler was playing and he began to jump up and down and breathe fire on Mederic, so that his eyebrows were burnt off and his hair singed. But the fiddler would not stop, he kept on playing backwards as if his life depended on it. The devil howled and screamed but it was too late. The fiddler came to the end of his tunes, threw down his fiddle and ran for his life, home to his wife and children who were there just as he had left them.

He never touched a fiddle again, although it is said that his youngest son became a great fiddler."

The Bridge to Halifax

The boy woke up just as the sun was coming up over the sea. The night had not entirely gone away yet. His room was still melancholy with the remnants of the dark. He dressed silently and pulled his bag out from underneath the bed. Then he crept downstairs, being careful not to let the stairboards squeak.

He left his bag on the porch of the Presbytery and went straight to the barn to do the morning chores. With any luck, no one would notice he was gone until at least nine o'clock, perhaps not until High Mass at ten-thirty. By then, he would be across the bridge at Margaree Harbour beyond the limits of the parish. Perhaps someone would give him a lift after that and he would ride all the way to Canso.

The boy's notion of the island beyond the boundaries of the village was sketchy. He knew that to the North, there was Cheticamp. Cheticamp was a town. It had a Main Street with some stores and up from the harbour, there was a high school and a small hospital. St. Joseph de la Mer had none of these things.

When Daniel went to Cheticamp with Father Aucoin, the boys who hung around the Main Street looked at his clothes as if there were a big sign on them which blinked and said, "St. Joseph de la Mer, St. Joseph de la Mer." He didn't say much. He just followed Father Aucoin around, who had a certain route. First, he visited the government man and the two men talked in the kitchen. The government man was from Quebec City and talked with a funny accent. The priest always had a complaint about the government.

Then they went around to the hospital and from the hospital, they went to see Father Cormier in the Presbytery which was so grand your footsteps echoed when you walked in the front door. When they arrived at the Presbytery, he was given a list and sent to the store to buy a few things for Mrs. Cross. It was here the Cheticamp boys were waiting for him. Once, one of them tripped him and he went sprawling face first onto the floor. He managed to do it quite silently. He scrambled to his feet almost as soon as he had fallen, only his hands and pride scraped. The Cheticamp boys were all smiles. "*Eh bien, le garçon du prêtre,*" they said, as if this was a big discovery.

"*Il est de la Mer*," another one said.

They laughed.

The boy felt his ears burn. His brother would have known what to do. He would have walked over and grabbed one of those smiling faces by the shirt with one hand and hit him with the other. The fight would have been short and furious. His brother would have won. He always did. But Daniel was not built along the same lines. The behaviour of the boys disconcerted him. He thought vaguely that perhaps there was something wrong with him. He did not understand the rules in Cheticamp. Perhaps he had done something wrong. He stood up and dusted himself off and then fished around in his pocket for the list that the priest had given him.

Father Aucoin picked him up in front of the store in the buggy and they drove quickly back to the village, the steel shoes of the horse striking sparks against the stones as he trotted along. The boy was relieved to be leaving. He did not like Cheticamp. No, when he ran away, it would be to the south, towards Canso and Halifax.

Canso and Halifax, those two names were all he really knew of what lay south of the village. He knew the island was fairly big and there was a place called Baddeck, but it all blended in. He had no real notion if Canso came first or Baddeck came first or even if one was on the way to the other. He'd never been beyond the Margaree River which framed the southern boundary of the village.

Margaree Harbour had a long, narrow wooden bridge across the mouth of the river. Beyond the wooden bridge was Canso where he could catch the ferry to the mainland. On the mainland, he would find Halifax where his brother was living. They would live together just as they had done before either had gone to the Presbytery. It seemed simple enough. Simpler than going to Cheticamp where people would know he was the priest's boy and he would be returned to the Presbytery.

No, the place to go was Halifax. Halifax was like Boston. People disappeared into Boston and they never came back.

He pitchforked bundles of thick, sweet-smelling hay into the mangers of the cows, the calves and the roan horse. Then he cleaned the gutters of manure and sprinkled some sawdust until the floor was pleasant smelling. Everything was ready for Mrs. Cross. The housekeeper would suspect nothing when she came out to milk. By the time the priest discovered that he was gone, it would be too late, he would be beyond Margaree Harbour.

The early morning sunlight filtered silently through the upper windows of the barn in long, angled beams. Everything was exactly as it should be. The boy set his pitchfork in the rack and left, latching the stable door carefully behind him. The fullness of summer had descended on the island. Spiders' cobwebs glinted in the grass and the lazy sense of a day arriving perfectly was everywhere. He picked up his canvas bag from the presbytery porch and walked quietly down to the road which would take him to Margaree Harbour.

A tiny brown mouse came skittering out of the grass at the edge of the road, ran a comical circle around the boy and then launched himself in a comical zig zag towards the other side of the road. The mouse was so small that he had to imagine his legs and then the ball of fur was gone into the long grass at the other side of the road. The boy waited for another sequence in the little drama, but nothing happened, no fox appeared in hot pursuit, no hawk came sweeping down from the sky to pounce.

The boy decided to take this as a good omen. The mouse was free to go and so was he. For a brief second, he thought of going home and then discarded it. His father would wallop him and send him straight back to the Presbytery; that was sure. He was always greeted at home with a confusing mixture of respect and anger that always left the boy upset and shaken until he stopped visiting his home. If he complained, it was always the same response, the same speech, the same exasperation in his father's voice.

"Do you know how many parents would love to have their son in your shoes? Half the parish, that's who! I hear them all the time. 'Isn't Daniel doing well in school! Isn't Daniel doing well at the piano!' Everytime I go to church, it's the same thing. What they're really saying is 'Why can't it be my son who lives at the Presbytery? Why does it always have to be a Boudreau boy?'"

"Because Mama is dead!" Daniel wanted to yell back at his father, but there were some things that you did not say to fathers. The boy bit the inside of his lip and ate his soup.

The only sound for a long time was their spoons hitting the bowls. There was a poisonous feeling in the air. A feeling which the boy did not understand. All he had said was he wanted to come home. He had thought his father would be pleased, instead it felt as if his father had been waiting for him to complain, as if it was his fault Mama was dead.

He never said anything again. He went back to the Presbytery, did his evening chores quietly, practised his piano pieces, and promptly went to bed. The days went by in a bleak way. Father Aucoin was pleased with him because he no longer asked impertinent questions. He did not disappear with Ulric à Arthur to play hide and seek. He did not arrive late and out of breath for Mass. But all the time, the thought kept going round in his head that he could not go home; that his father did not want him. He must stay at the Presbytery and do as he was told.

It was then he began to think of running away to Halifax. Halifax was so far away that no one would think to send him back. The priest would get a new boy to do the chores and that would be that. He would be free of Father Aucoin and Father Aucoin would be free of him.

The boy was walking quickly by the most beautiful part of the village. Here the valley was quite large and the fields were dotted with cows. A clear stream flowed through the middle and in the distance the great green mountains of the Highlands flowed into the blue of the sky. Save for the rustle of a breeze from the sea, there was not a sound. Even the birds had not quite shaken themselves awake. The village was still deep asleep in its Sunday morning reverie. It was as if the boy was walking through a painting composed by some romantic but the boy saw nothing of this, he did not look up from his thoughts until he had walked past all the familiar landmarks, until he had entered a part of the parish which he did not know well.

The southern edge of the parish was not populated with neat clusters of houses and barns laid out in long, regular rows. Here, the coast was jagged with great cliffs plunging straight down to the sea. There was no harbour, no gently sloping landscape. Here the escarpment narrowed and the farms were hidden from the sea wind behind steep bluffs. All ease was gone, instead the landscape looked bitter and hard. The boy's pace did not slow, but he began to wonder how far it was to Canso. Perhaps someone would give him a ride when he got to the bridge at Margaree.

Then he began to hear the priest's voice. He and Philibert were arguing again. He had fallen asleep last night with their voices rising through the grating in his bedroom floor. Sometimes, their voices were loud and clear, other times faint and far away. Bits and pieces often came back to him in the morning like odd fragments of a vivid dream. The priest's voice strident and hard like a twitch across his shoulders.

"Don't you dare lecture me, Philibert. You could have gone to university. You could have made something of yourself and what are you? The village clown. Nothing more than the village clown."

"Less praying and more laughter would not hurt you, cousin."

"And don't call me cousin. You do it just to irritate me."

"Ah, now the truth is out. I'm not respectful enough, that's what bothers you about your cousin Philibert and that's what bothers you about the boy. What should we do? Bow down in front of you like a plaster statue of the Virgin Mary? Should I start calling you the Virgin Aucoin?"

"As usual, you take everything to extremes."

"Well, how do you want us all to be? Hypocrites like Charles à Martin who sits right up front and mumbles faithfully over his rosary? At mass, on Sunday, he's a model of church piety and in the afternoon, he beats his wife and children."

"What has Charles à Martin got to do with Daniel?"

"Everything in the world, you've got to have eyes in your head as well as prayers on your lips to deal with people. So the kid is a ragamuffin and a pain in the ass, which I admit he can be, but he isn't mean or deceptive. He's just got the guts to get into good, honest trouble."

"We get a photographer in the village once a year and we get one photograph of the class. One souvenir of the year and Daniel sticks his tongue out. Every parent in the entire parish will look at that photograph and say, "Oh, yes, the boy sitting in the front with his tongue out, that's Daniel Boudreau, the priest's boy."

"Let them."

"I would chastise any other child who did it, but I should ignore the behaviour of my own altar boy?"

"Cousin, I don't understand how any man who is so smart can be so dumb. People aren't turnips, you can't mash them all into the same shape. What works for one, doesn't work for another."

The boy had heard them argue too many times to pay much attention to the words. In a curious way, he found it comforting. The priest's voice was forceful, clear. Philibert's voice was softer, even when he was angry, there seemed to be a smile in his voice as if even he could not take himself seriously.

Neither one ever agreed with the other. After a while, it began to seem to the boy as if the two men were standing at different windows of the Presbytery, looking at the same scene, but neither would leave his window to come and look through the other's window and so they settled on yelling at one another.

The boy did not understand it. In public, they were perfectly civil to each other. Philibert always doffed his cap respectfully in the priest's direction and Father Aucoin would briefly acknowledge his disreputable cousin.

Philibert had been trying to protect him last night. He had remembered that, but it was all mixed up with the argument about sin and Philibert, who was not the purest of men, and Charles à Martin who beat his children. If he were the priest, he would not let Charles à Martin inside the church for two seconds. He would send him directly to hell.

The road curved around a headland and he finally saw the bridge across the Margaree. It was a good sight and for the first time since he had woken the beauty of the day sank into him. The sky was clear with small pillow clouds drifting along. In the distance, he could hear the sound of the sea drifting in and out against the cliffs. When he got to Halifax, he would tell his brother all about it, and Robert would tell him stories about the days when he had been the priest's boy.

Robert had always gotten along with Father Aucoin. But then, Robert always got along. He knew how to lie. He said he was visiting Aunt Isabet when he was visiting girls and Robert had gotten away with it. The priest was telling him what a fine young man Robert was; how he expected great things from Robert.

Robert was okay, but he could not play the piano to save his life. When he was ten, he, Daniel, could play as well as Robert could at eighteen. On the other hand, Robert did not stick out his tongue at the photographer. He stood with his arms folded in the back row resolutely staring out at the photographer, blank-faced like all the other kids.

When no one was around, Daniel would often stare back at the photographs which hung in the hallway of the Presbytery. They were all there, pictures of every priest of St. Joseph de la Mer, pictures from the school-house, pictures of all the choirs that Father Aucoin had led. He studied them all. They looked mysterious to the boy. He could remember the day that they had taken the picture of Robert's class. But Robert looked only vaguely like his brothers. If you looked closely, you could see the Boudreau family stamp, curly brown hair, blue eyes and a long, thin nose. But mostly, his brother looked stupid and blank-faced as if fear of being exposed to the occasion for sin had turned his face into stone.

The picture that Elodie and he were in had been taken around the steps of the school. Elodie was standing at the edge of the group. She was the tallest girl. She seemed to be staring directly at Daniel, but from a long, unreachable distance as if she was on one planet and he on another. One time, he stared at the photograph of Elodie for so long, he began to see the girl in the photograph fly apart. The little black and white dots separated from each other one after another until there was no more Elodie, no more school-house, no more rows of boys and girls. The little black and white dots rose like snow up the stairwell of the presbytery, one after another, until there was no photograph left, nothing but a dirty white square where the rows of blank faces had once been.

He hadn't wanted to be melted down into little black and white dots and hung on the wall. He had not wanted to be frozen next to Elodie, forever close to her, forever not touching, forever worried about the occasion for sin. He stuck his tongue out. The shutter went click. The dots were frozen.

Father Aucoin said he had ruined the photograph; that all the boys and girls had gotten their hair washed and brushed; that they were wearing their best clothes and he had made fun of them all; that he had been thoughtless and selfish. He must start thinking about other people besides himself, otherwise he would end up stupid like Philibert, the matchmaker.

Philibert had never amounted to anything because he had no faith in anything but his next meal. The same thing would happen to him. He would become a junk piano player entertaining drunk people. People got stupider or smarter, that was a favourite expression of Father Aucoin. There was no in between.

The bridge to Halifax wasn't far away now. The sun was warm against the boy's sweater. He began to walk down the hill towards the Margaree River. Maybe, he would become a junk piano player. One thing for sure, his brother never would. He wasn't good enough. He needed the notes written down.

A horse and buggy came trotting swiftly over the rise and before the boy could move, the priest was pulling up beside him.

"Where are you going, Daniel?"

The boy squinted up at the priest, trying to gauge how much trouble he was in. "To Halifax. To see my brother."

"You're twelve, Daniel. Twelve-year-olds do not walk to Halifax."

"I'm almost thirteen."

"Yes," said the priest, and he stared out towards the bridge as if he was considering this. He did not seem angry, which surprised the boy.

"Perhaps, when you're thirteen. Right now, we've got a Mass to serve. People will be wondering where we are. You'd better get in."

There was no choice in the priest's voice.

The boy got in the buggy. Father Aucoin clacked the reins over the horse's back and the horse began to pull them back towards St. Joseph de la Mer. Daniel turned and over his shoulder caught a glimpse of the bridge across the Margaree disappear.

Reds and Blues

Grandfather was not a great fan of Albert à Didier. They tolerated each other in public places, but Albert à Didier did not step on Grandfather's farm and Grandfather had never once stepped in the hotel of Albert à Didier. Grandfather would not even drink beer for fear he might be lining the pockets of Albert à Didier. Grandfather was a life-long supporter of the noble Mr. McKenzie-King and the Liberal Party of Canada. Albert à Didier was misguided, avaricious and deceitful which is to say, he was a Tory. When Grandfather was feeling particularly cranky at the world, he would think of Albert à Didier and he would be obliged to split wood to calm down. Eventually, this would cheer him up, as there is nothing quite like the contemplation of evil to stoke the fires of virtuous content.

With each stroke of the axe, Grandfather recalled the many sins of Albert à Didier and there were a lot. They went right back to the days when they had been boys together on the pick and shovel gang that had hacked the first Trail out through the Park. At nineteen, Albert à Didier was already plotting.

One Saturday afternoon, when they were working on the Trail, Albert organised a contest between John James McTavish and Grandfather to see who could shovel the most gravel in twenty minutes Now, it wasn't a contest that Grandfather would have chosen, for John James McTavish was the largest, strongest man on the crew and Grandfather was the slightest. But once it was arranged, Grandfather would not withdraw.

The two men stripped to the waist. The foreman's whistle sounded and away they went. John James started faster than Grandfather, his pick and shovel going like a whirlwind. Smash, shovel, smash, shovel. Grandfather trailed along behind him going as fast as he could, but he was not as big or as strong as John James and it seemed clear enough who would win. But as the two carts began to fill, John James slowed down, and began to take "breathers." Now, Grandfather may have been small, but he was all muscle and bone. He kept right on swinging and shovelling at exactly the same pace that he had started. When John James was taking another one of his "breathers," he caught up and passed him before the bigger man realised it had happened. Then John James began to fly again. Sweat flew off the men's bare backs. Their supporters cheered each man on. Grandfather, sensing that John James was catching him, his heart pounding in his chest, found the strength to accelerate. He did not look either to the right or left, he just shovelled and threw, shovelled and threw. The whistle went and the foreman pronounced William Doucet's cart full, a few strokes ahead of John McTavish.

The boys from St. Joseph de la Mer went home triumphant and everywhere the story went up and down the coast that little William Doucet had beaten Big John McTavish. Everyone that is except Albert à Didier who had lost a week's wages because he had bet on John McTavish to win.

Now, when Grandfather started that far back with the sins of Albert à Didier, you knew he would be at the wood pile for a good long time before he could work himself up to the present cabals. I left him alone to plot the downfall of Albert à Didier, for it was one thing to plot the demise of Albert à Didier, and another thing to do it.

Albert à Didier was a rich man. He owned the only house that passed for a hotel in the village. He owned a large flock of sheep on Cheticamp Island. He had timber concessions up in the Highlands. Money moved through his fingers. Money was the reason he had fought Father Aucoin and the Credit Union so hard. He had understood immediately that a Credit Union would threaten his money-lending and he was right.

Albert à Didier liked to control. His boat, *La Chanceux*, never caught a fish; instead, it made regular trips for rum to St. Pierre et Miquelon. When the Blues won the election, it was Albert à Didier who informed my uncles that their trucks would no longer be required on provincial road crews. There was nothing that happened in the village that Albert à Didier did not have his sticky fingers in. He was '*l'homme fort du French Shore.*'

When Grandfather had finally chopped enough wood to dim the memories of Albert à Didier's many victories, he came in the house to eat his Sunday dinner. He said nothing to anyone. He seemed to have run out of preaching wrath, but he had devised a plan to scupper Albert à Didier.

At dusk, without a word of explanation, he saddled up the old mare and rode down to the harbour. He wore three sweaters and took the heaviest wool blanket in the house. He tied the mare up out of sight behind the hill and then sat down to quietly wait for *La Chanceux* to come stealing into the harbour from St. Pierre et Miquelon.

She did not arrive and he came home at dawn cranky and too tired to do the morning chores. The next night, he went down to the harbour again. He waited in vain. There was still no sign of *La Chanceux*. For five nights in a row, he rode down to the harbour and waited until his eyes began to sink in his head and he grew hollow-cheeked and stubble-faced. Grandfather, who was always a garrulous, cheery man, grew silent and cross. During the day, he did his chores in a blur of fatigue and at night wrapped in his blanket, he would nod in a dozy, uncomfortable sleep.

When *La Chanceux* finally did arrive, she slipped silently into the harbour in the pitch of night without running lights, so quietly that Grandfather did not see or hear her. He was sleeping quietly under the tree wrapped in his blanket and wool sweaters. *La Chanceux* was tied up at Albert à Didier's wharf with scarcely a ripple. They were rolling the last barrels of rum onto a waiting truck before Grandfather realised what was happening.

Now, the practice was always to unload the rum and then hide it somewhere safe from prying Liberals until the eve of the election. No one but a tried and true Blue ever knew where they were hidden. Then before the votes were being cast, the barrels would be rolled out and free rum would begin circulating through the village courtesy of the Conservative Party of Canada and Albert à Didier.

The truck pulled away from the dock with her barrels of rum safely stowed behind the tailgate. Grandfather jumped on his horse and rode for his life after the truck as it bumped along the narrow road beside the salt pond. The truck went all the way to the head of the pond. The hiding place, to Grandfather's amazement, turned out to be in the sawdust of his own son's sawmill. Grandfather tied his horse up safely out of sight from the six men and crept forward in time to watch Albert à Didier covering his barrels of rum up in the hills of sawdust that were always piled at the end of the saw. What safer place to hide the rum than in the sawdust of a good Liberal business? Who would have thought?

In the dead of night, he went looking for some tried and true Liberals.

Grandfather got home at sun-up and fell into the first deep sleep he had had in a week. He did not wake until noon and when he did, he said nothing. He just washed, shaved and went out to attend the farm chores with not a word to anyone.

Two days before the election, the rum from St. Pierre began to circulate in the village, free, courtesy of the Liberal Party of Canada and William Doucet. Grandfather explained this was perfectly correct because red was the colour of justice, road contracts, noble aspirations and the Liberal Party of Canada.

The Seal Hunt

"Play an A, Daniel."

Daniel sounded the A note.

"Did you all hear that?" called Father Aucoin from the front of the choir. "Now sing it for me, A-A-A. First the sopranos, then the tenors, now the basses."

The choir sang A.

"That's better, much better. Shall we try it again? Ready, Daniel?"

Father Aucoin beat out the three preparatory notes and they began: "Gloria, gloria, glo-o-oria, in excelsis deo."

This time, the tenors and basses counterpointed the sopranos perfectly and the Glorias rose to heaven in exactly spaced waves. It made the hair stand up on the back of Daniel's neck.

"Not so loud, Daniel. Don't drown the choir. I want to hear you together."

Father Aucoin tapped his music stand twice and it was over, the choir dispersed. The sound of their voices fading into the shadows of the ceiling. The church was empty and silent. It floated on alone. Only the two boys remained. They sat quietly behind the organ, Ulric on a stool and Daniel on the floor with his knees pulled up under his chin. It was a warm, small corner of the church, impossible to approach without being observed.

It was Ulric's job to pump the organ during choir practice and Daniel's to play.

Ulric passed Daniel some spruce gum and the two boys chewed in companionable silence as the bitter-sweet sap pulled pleasantly at their teeth.

"It's good stuff," said Daniel, taking a large, ugly wad out of his mouth to examine it. "Where did you get it?"

"The tree by the spring," said Ulric cryptically. "There's always good gum on the south side."

"You know, I'd like just once in my life, just once, to get through a choir practice without the priest telling me that I play too loud. An organ is not a piano. You can't play it like it didn't have pipes."

"He doesn't mean any harm."

"I hate it. He should get someone else to play."

"Who?"

"I don't know. Someone who is good at saying, 'yes, Father Aucoin.'"

"Maybe Aunt Isabet."

"She can't play."

"She can play a little. I've heard her."

"Do you hear something?" Daniel stood up and peered around the corner of the organ. The church seemed empty. He walked quietly out onto the gallery where he could see down to the floor of the church. Through the tall, narrow windows, the late afternoon sun bathed the little church in multi-coloured light. Dust motes rose lazily inside the beams of light. For a moment, Daniel had the uneasiest feeling, as if he was falling; that years and years were sweeping by in a few seconds; his mother was alive; his mother was dead; he was the priest's boy; he was not the priest's boy; he was staring into the photograph of himself except he was not himself; he was someone else. The feeling bled out of him like blood leaving him weak and dizzy.

"What is it?"

"I thought I heard Father Aucoin in the sacristy."

"He's gone for tea," said Ulric, but he was also whispering.

"Your brother will stop for me in the morning?" asked Daniel.

"I've told you ten times that he will," said Ulric. "And if my brother says he'll do something, he does it."

"Okay, okay, I'm sorry," said Daniel, realising that he was irritating his best friend. "Pump the organ for me, will you, Ulric?"

"Why?"

"I'd like to play once more before I go. It will be a while before I play again. I want to play to suit myself."

"Okay, but not too long. I've got to get home."

Daniel sat down at the organ. The keyboard was quite small. A few rows of keys, they hardly looked like anything at all. Daniel set his hands down upon them and began to play. His hands moved rapidly without hesitation. He did not read any music. It came from inside him, chord after chord crashed out in crescendo after crescendo until the church windows rattled and it began to sound as if there was a sea storm in the church. Ulric raced to keep up with him, and both boys forgot everything but the voice of the organ.

Neither boy noticed the priest appear. He entered from the side door and strode quickly down the centre aisle and up the stairs taking the steps two at a time to the gallery. His hand touched Daniel's shoulder and the boy jumped up from the keyboard, the music dying as he did so.

"What are you doing, Daniel? Trying to murder our old organ?"

"No," said the boy, but he was trembling.

"It sounds like it."

"Why can't I ever play the way I want to?" asked the boy, his voice tense and rising.

"What music is it that you're playing?"

"My own."

"Since when did Daniel Boudreau become a composer?" asked the priest, sitting down at the keyboard. "This is music," and a calm, celestial sound began to fill the church. "Do you recognise it?"

"Bach," said the boy.

"Correct, Johann Sebastian Bach. He was a composer. You're not. You were just making noise."

The boy's face was white and he stood very still. He looked like he wished to spit at the priest."

The priest stopped playing and saw the look on the boy's face.

"You do have talent, Daniel. I never thought I'd say this, but you're even better than your brother Robert. He was quick to learn, but he did not have your touch. Sometimes, when I hear you playing, I just stop and listen. It sounds perfect."

A little colour began to return to the boy's cheeks.

"But that wasn't music you were playing. It was a temper tantrum you were having. You were punching the keys, not playing them." The priest stood up from the bench.

"Ulric, thank you for pumping today. If you wish to stop by for supper, you may." And the priest was gone, down the narrow stairs and out the front door.

The church returned to silence. Ulric emerged from the side of the organ chewing on an enormous wad of spruce gum.

"He sure was mad," said Ulric comfortably biting down on his gum.

"He's always angry."

"Maybe you should think this thing over," said Ulric.

"What thing?"

"The seal hunt."

"I'm going."

"Cabin boys don't make much money. It's not as if you were out on the ice. You won't get a percentage of the catch or anything. You'll just get a few dollars for cleaning tables and washing dishes."

"Are you coming to the Presbytery for supper?"

"No."

"And you tell me I shouldn't leave."

"I've got to get home."

"Bullshit, Ulric. You just don't want to come."

Ulric took his gum out. "You'll miss the school exams."

"I'll be at the edge of the road at six tomorrow. This time he won't catch me. I'll be in Sydney before he knows I'm gone."

"Cars offer the occasion for sin," said Ulric, mimicking the priest.

Both boys grinned.

In his mind, the boy could see the priest bursting through the front doors of the Presbytery. The sun would be just coming up from behind the sea. He would be calling 'Daniel! Daniel! Come back!"

But it would be too late. He was free.

Philibert Goes to Heaven

Did you ever notice that people remember failure better than success? Wherever I go, it's always the same story. Wonderful goes with the meat and potatoes, failure with dessert. The soup has barely hit the table and I'm told that the eldest son has just married a lovely girl. It was a marriage like no other. The bride looked wonderful. She was dressed all in white. The groom was as handsome as could be. We finish the soup with the mother's eyes glistening at thoughts of her son's marriage.

The soup is cleared away.

Monsieur tells me that he had a fine harvest this year. The barn is full of dry, sweet-smelling hay. He received a good price for his summer cattle. The Mrs. nods her head in agreement when her husband speaks and we all eat our meat and potatoes to the tune of a farm report.

Then the dessert arrives.

The husband leaves the room and the Mrs. tells me with deep regret in her voice that her first husband, a tall, handsome man, was drowned in a storm, not a mile from the harbour. Her second husband drinks too much, that's why the kitchen is painted blue instead of white. He got drunk and mixed the blue paint with the white. When he gets one drink in him, he can't seem to stop until the bottle's gone. Then, there's the daughter who went to the Boston States. Her mother did not want her to go. They had an argument. She had an operation last year, but the Mrs. doesn't know what it was for, the daughter never writes. It's these stories that the Mrs. dwells on like beautiful stones, she can never stop polishing.

The tragedies vary, but not the love of them. My old friend, Marcel Boudreau, has six sons. One of them works in Ottawa. One is a doctor. Another runs the saw mill at Margaree Forks. Another has a big fishing boat in Cheticamp and makes more money than you can imagine. The fifth is a great fiddler. They are all busy, successful men. Their houses are full of comings and goings. Marcel has their pictures hanging on the wall. Pictures of his boys graduating, pictures of the boys getting married, pictures of the grandchildren, but who does he talk about? It's always the youngest, Daniel, the one who ran away. I can see Marcel now. He will sigh and look at the faded picture of Daniel in the surplice of an altar boy. Then he will say, "but Daniel was the smartest." Then he will sigh again, and say, "even Father Aucoin said he was the smartest."

Marcel blames himself, that's who he grieves over, the youngest. Daniel was only five when his mother died. He never got over her death. He didn't fit in at the Presbytery. He and Father Aucoin didn't get along. Daniel could never do anything right. It was comical, really, because they were alike as two peas in a pod. I could see Daniel being exactly the same type of priest as Father Aucoin. Daniel was the only person I ever saw who could correct my cousin at the piano and live to tell the tale.

Marcel blames himself. He blames himself for the boy and he blames himself for his wife's death. Those are the two stones Marcel wears in his shoes and he's been so busy polishing them all these years, he's never had time to remarry. He'll never admit this, but after Marie died, he decided if God wasn't going to put Marcel Boudreau into Purgatory right away, then he'd do the job for him. So there he was, a tall, strapping man with dark hair and a flashing smile, alone. He cooked his own meals. Went to church by himself. I'd be a rich man today if I'd received a dollar for every time a woman said to me, "I'd like to meet Marcel Boudreau."

Of course, it's natural to grieve. Who wouldn't? Marie was wise and beautiful. I loved her myself. But people die before their time, it happens. If it didn't there would be no widows and who would need a Matchmaker?

I arranged three marriages for Peter Delaney before he was twenty-five. He was twenty when he married the first time. His first wife caught pneumonia and died six months after they were married. They barely had time to get acquainted. A year later, I fixed him up with a young woman from Chimney Corners. A Scottish girl. Just as Gaelic as the day is long. Her family lived way up in the hills. She scarcely had a word of French or English.

She had seen Peter when he was driving the taxi from Cheticamp to Baddeck and taken a shine to him. I couldn't see how it was going to work out myself. She spoke Gaelic and Peter spoke French, but it didn't seem to bother them at all. Peter liked her right off and they lived happily ever after. Except happily ever after turned out to be pretty short. She died with their first child. The baby died too. So there was Peter, all of twenty-three years, married twice and nothing to show for it.

I lost track of him after that and I think for a time he lost track of himself. Anyway, he surfaced a few years later and I fixed him up with Monique Poirier from Grand Etang. This time, it took. They had a dozen kids and Peter became what Father Aucoin used to call a pillar of the community. He worked so hard, I'm surprised he ever had time to make kids.

But what do I remember? What does Philibert, the Matchmaker remember? Not Monique Poirier and her twelve, happy children, no, not a bit of it. I remember the second wife. She had freckles and reddish hair. She was what the Scots call 'a bonnie girl.' She was waiting for me at her father's house. All she had was a sailor's canvas bag. She kissed her parents goodbye as if she were walking around the corner instead of down the mountainside to meet her new husband. When I walked down the mountain with her to meet Peter, she would not stop chattering. She was as full of life as one can be. I only understood half of what she said, but that didn't stop her. She was sure my few words of Gaelic were the equal of a whole dictionary.

I often think of that Scottish girl. Sometimes, I dream about her. I can see her clear as clear. It's not sensible, I know, but I blame myself. If I hadn't mentioned the Scottish girl to Peter Delaney, he would not have noticed her, and if he hadn't noticed her, they wouldn't have gotten married.

You would think I would have learned, but I didn't. If the Pope could be infallible, so could Philibert the Matchmaker. I'm sure I gave as much advice around the kitchen table as my cousin ever did in his confessional. The only difference was, instead of saying penance, you had to give me a few pennies; that was your penance; pennies for Philibert, Hail Marys for Father Aucoin.

Bah! That was a long time ago. I don't give advice any longer. I've retired. If you want to collect stones in your shoes, then you can place them by yourself. You don't need my help. I'm not like my cousin. May he rest in peace. I have no magic formula that's going to get anyone to heaven.

Yes, a smart man, sure enough. There was no one who could play the organ like Father Aucoin, but I'm not sure he knew shit from shinola. Ah, don't get your knickers in a twist. He's my cousin and I'll say what I want about him. I did to his face so why shouldn't I now, now he's gone?

Sure, sure, I know he did good things, more than most people know. I didn't find out myself until he died that he gave two thousand dollars to get the Credit Union started. And the Credit Union was the start of the Fishermen's Co-op and just about everything else in the village. But I know where he got the money. He got it from his brother. His brother would send him money from time to time for this and that. I was there once when he got a cheque to buy himself a car. It was a cheque for three hundred dollars. I'd never seen that much money before; it made quite an impression. I remember Father Aucoin laughing when he read the letter. He said to me, "How can I buy a car when half of my parishioners can barely put shoes on their children's feet?"

Easy as pie, I told him. Your brother sent you the money for a car, buy a car, that was my advice. I was ready to go to Halifax and get him a Chevy.

My sainted cousin also did more harm than most people know. I used to spend half my time trying to patch up his blunders. Sometimes I could and sometimes I couldn't. Remember the time, he preached against Dulcine Leblanc for not 'avoiding the occasion for sin'?

Let me tell you, that wasn't pretty. There she was, completely alone in the world. Her brothers and sisters had all moved away. Her parents who were ancient and without two pennies to their name died leaving her nothing but a harbour shack and my good cousin got her fired from her job at the hospital in Cheticamp. It was the only job she ever had in the village. That was a wonderful thing, let me tell you. Just wonderful. No one would talk to her. She lived alone for months on a few people's charity. Finally, in the dead of winter, William Doucet was obliged to drive her to Inverness and put her on the train for Boston with nothing but one cardboard suitcase and a few dollars in her pocket. I could have throttled my sainted cousin.

Another time, I was invited to a house, not far from here and found this young man beside himself with rage and despair. He'd fallen in love with a young widow from Cheticamp and had asked her to marry him. She had agreed. I had nothing to do with it. The two had met and fallen in love all by themselves. This is a constant surprise to me, the way people decide that they are in love. It seems the most arbitrary thing in the world. One day, they're walking along minding their own business, the next day, they're in love.

Anyway, the two of them had fallen in love and the young man had gone off happily to see Father Aucoin to arrange for the reading of the banns. Well, he finds my good cousin teaching some child how to hammer out her scales and he waits patiently in the kitchen for the lesson to end. Eventually, the priest appears. The young man explains that he has found the love-of-his-life and he would like Father Aucoin to read the banns at High Mass.

My cousin agrees immediately, for the young man is from a fine family. Father Aucoin knows him well and would put him firmly on the improving side of the Parish register.

"And what is the name of the girl?" asks my cousin with his fountain pen cocked, ready to record her pedigree in the parish register.

The young man tells Father Aucoin her name and explains that she is a young widow who lives just over the parish line in Cheticamp with three small children.

The pen freezes in my cousin's hand. His lips tighten. His eyes narrow. Father Aucoin is not pleased. He looks away from the young man. Puts his fountain pen down on the desk. He begins to drum his fingers lightly against his knees. A sure sign that he is displeased. Finally, Father Aucoin tells the young man in the voice he reserves for God.

"I think you should reconsider. You deserve better."

The young man is so shocked he can barely muster the voice to protest. All he can hear are the words, "I think you should reconsider. You deserve better."

There is a long, long silence in the room. For the young man, it feels like he has been plunged to the bottom of the pond and is having trouble surfacing.

When my cousin sees that he has shocked the young man, he explain, "I've met this woman. She can barely read. She was married at eighteen. She's had children like a rabbit. She's older than you are. Let her find someone more suitable to her station in life."

The young man left the presbytery as if someone had shot him. Here was the man who had taught him catechism; the man he had served as an altar boy; whom he regarded as highly as his own father, telling him that the woman he wished to marry was not suitable to his station in life.

I found the young man a day or so later in the most terrible despair. His parents did not know what to do. One minute, he was shedding tears of rage at Father Aucoin and the next he was feeling ashamed of himself for falling in love with a woman 'beneath his station in life.' After all, Father Aucoin was a man who knows.

In those days I was sure that Father Aucoin did not know everything. So I told the lad as delicately as possible, for the young man was in an excited state, that my good cousin didn't know shit from shinola, and furthermore that the love-of-his-life was an exceptionally fine woman and he should get himself to Cheticamp as quickly as possible, marry the lady at St. Pierre, not here at de la Mer, and live happily ever after.

Which is exactly what he did. They got married in Cheticamp and had three more children. A happier, more saintly family would be hard to find. That was one of my successes.

Marcel Boudreau, on the other hand, I count as a failure. He eventually became a stone in my own shoe. No matter what I said. No matter how many times I visited Marcel was determined to be inconsolable.

He had decided that his wife's death was his fault and therefore he should be punished. In a way, he was right. Marie Boudreau died of T.B. and too many babies. She had eight children in eight years, six lived and two died. It wore her out.

Yes, yes, I know it takes two people to make a baby, but there are ways to control how many babies you make and neither Marcel or Dr. Seveau had the guts to go against the Gospel according to Father Aucoin, that's the long and short of it. Sure, I blame Marcel. I blame Dr. Seveau too. He had about as much fibre as wet grass.

Anyway, it was all very sad. Marie died at thirty-two. Thirty-two! And Marcel carried out his own trial, was his own prosecutor, judge and jury, convicted himself and never slept with another woman. That was his punishment.

Two wrongs never make a right and they didn't this time either. After Marie died, I'm sure that the boy must have felt some of his father's anger at the church and himself. I think the older boys understood, but not Daniel. When I took him to the Presbytery to be the priest's boy, I thought he would grow out of it. I was sure he would get along with Father Aucoin just as his older brother had, but it didn't work out. The anger stayed and set down roots in the boy's soul.

In the end we all get condemned for some crime or other. My cousin thought we all could be saints. I'm convinced we're all criminals. I don't know exactly what I've been convicted of, God knows there's enough to choose from, but I know what my punishment is, I've been condemned to glimpse heaven. Fortunately, it's not playing a harp somewhere beyond the clouds.

Heaven was walking down the mountainside with the young Scottish girl. The snow was brilliant, white and light cascading around us with every step. The sky was so blue that you could feel the colour. Lights sparkled in the auburn hair of the Scottish girl. Her voice was the most wonderful music I have ever heard. It was so courageous, so filled with cheery determination to make a great success of her life. I still dream about that day.

I fell in love with the idea of life as it can be, but never is, as it is held out to us and is denied us. I was allowed for a few short moments to feel with my entire heart and then I was released to go back to my ordinary life. Yes, I fell in love with her, but not in the way you imagine, because I knew that it was as futile an affection as my cousin's infatuation with the Bible.

I think my sainted cousin received the same punishment with his vocation. He never talked about it, but I am sure that when he was a young man, the door was opened for him and he was allowed for a few seconds to get a brief glimpse of heaven. And he spent the rest of his life scrambling to pry the door back open; the punishment for my cousin was the harder he pried, the harder he prayed, the farther away heaven got, until in the end his heart gave out with trying.

I've never been quite sure whether he was magnificently stupid or just more courageous than I. He would not admit defeat, not for a second. He would have died first and in the end, I guess, he did. He was only fifty-three. So many people leaned on him that sometimes I think he did stupid things from nothing more than fatigue. He had no wife. No one to help sustain him except the circulars from the Bishop which always said the same thing, 'buck up, pray more and stay away from Credit Unions.' He felt remorse. I know that. He felt remorse about Dulcine Leblanc. He knew he'd done an evil thing, but he was trapped by his vision just as surely as I was trapped by mine.

I miss my cousin. There's no one to go to war against now.

End